AI

Lee Mae
Cassie Alexandra

Copyright ©2019 Lee Mae & Cassie Alexandra

Names, characters, and incidents depicted in this ebook are products of the authors' imagination or are used fictitiously. Any resemblance to actual events, locales, organizations, or persons, living or dead, is entirely coincidental.

The unauthorized reproduction or distribution of this, or any copyrighted work is illegal. If you would like to share this ebook with another person, purchase an additional copy for the recipient. If you're reading this ebook and didn't purchase it or it was not purchased for your use only, please return to publisher and purchase your own copy. File sharing is an international crime, prosecuted by the United States Department of Justice Division of Cyber Crimes, in partnership with Interpol.

Criminal copyright infringement, including infringement without monetary gain, is punishable by seizure of computers, up to five years in federal prison, and a fine of $250,000 per reported occurrence.

Thank you for respecting the hard work of these authors.

Prologue

Jordan followed Duke into the strip-joint, hopped up on adrenaline and anxiety. He'd been looking for Hailey, his runaway bride, for the last three years, and was following up on a tip that she'd been spotted working there. As much as he wanted to murder the ungrateful bitch for making him look like a fool, part of him still wanted her. Would *always* want her. And by God, no matter what happened, he would take what was owed to him. He only hoped that she was still a virgin so he could at least have the satisfaction of being her first... and last.

He looked around. The seedy bar made his skin crawl. It was pleasing to know she'd had to resort to such a shitty place. He imagined that she'd been foolish enough to think he'd never find her in such a hick-town, waiting tables at the Triple B, which apparently stood for Beer, Boobs, and Barbecue. The place was a complete dive, reeking of beer, dirty ashtrays, and sex.

"Damn, look at the cha-chas on her," Duke, his best friend and head of clan security, said over the loud rock music.

Jordan glanced toward the stage. It was surrounded by rednecks who were hootin' and hollering at the bountiful stripper currently stuffing bills into a silver thong. As dirty as the place was, even he had to admit, the women were fuckable. Of course, he was part wolf and quite literally, a perpetual horn-dog.

Usually.

His sex-drive wasn't what it used to be. Not in the last few months, at least. Sure, he'd get an erection, but sustaining it was another matter. The last couple of times he'd tried performing, the show had ended abruptly. The women he'd been with, well, they hadn't complained, but he'd seen the look in their eyes. The disappointment.

Humiliated, he'd gotten his hands on some Viagra. It worked, but the fact of the matter was he shouldn't need help. Not when he was only twenty-eight and part beast. Virility was everything to a shifter. Knowing that he needed help, especially in the sex department, was horrifying.

It's because of Hailey.

Jordan was pretty confident that the bitch was to blame. Just thinking about Hailey, and all the things he wanted to do to her, gave him wood. He was pretty confident that there'd be no problems once he had her. She was both the problem and the cure for what ailed him.

Of course, there was the other thing. Something even more disturbing than losing an erection. Jordan was starting to have a hard time shifting. Twice he'd gotten stuck between canine and man, and it was painful as hell. Excruciating. It felt like he was being ripped apart. The inability to become fully man, or Lycan, lasted for no more than a few seconds, but it was enough to worry the shit out of him.

Unfortunately, he had to keep the problem a secret, too. He was in line to be the next Alpha and Jordan couldn't show any sign of weakness. Whatever was happening to him, he'd figure it out on his own. He had no choice.

"Boss?" Duke said, snapping him back to reality. "Where should we sit? Near the stage?"

"No. Toward the back. We need the element of surprise. She recognizes us and it's all over," Jordan replied.

"I thought that's why we're incognito."

They were both dressed up like bikers. Jordan even wore a long wig and fake beard, but Hailey was smart. Too smart. He didn't want to take any risks.

"She could still recognize one of us. She does and all of this was for nothing. We're not taking any chances."

Looking disappointed, Duke nodded and followed him to the back corner of the bar. The two sat down across from each other at a tall pub table, away from most eyes.

"You sure she's going to be here?" Jordan asked, checking out the waitress who was getting ready to head their way. The broad was a looker, with long red hair and legs up to the sky. She was a little on the skinny side, however, and Jordan preferred his women with more curves.

Like Hailey.

She was a natural beauty with a body he'd been craving ever since she'd turned fifteen. He'd wanted to take her then, but Travis, his father and the Alpha of his clan, had forbidden him to touch her until she was eighteen.

And his bride.

Being the Alpha's son, he'd had dibs on any female in the clan. She'd been the obvious choice. With her beauty and grace, everyone had wanted her. Even Duke.

Unfortunately, Hailey had been missing for three years, making her twenty-one now. She'd bolted without warning on the day of their wedding, bringing shame to the family. He knew he was the laughingstock of every Lycan clan, too. From Canada to Florida. It made his blood boil. Once he got his hands on her, Jordan vowed she'd pay for the humiliation she'd caused. One way or another.

Duke, watching the stage, nodded. "Yeah. My contact said she's here every Thursday night. Goes by the name of Amy."

"And, you're sure it's Hailey? I don't want to be wasting time here… in this dump," Jordan said, grimacing as his hand touched something sticky on the table.

"They have her picture. My guy is pretty sure she's the one."

He frowned. "Pretty sure?"

Duke shrugged. "Sure enough."

Jordan pinched the bridge of his nose. Hopefully they'd get lucky. He'd been following leads all over the Midwest, missing her every time. Either she was really crafty, or just plain lucky.

The waitress arrived and they ordered two beers.

"Did you want to order any ribs? They're on special tonight," she said.

"I'm a breast man myself," Duke said, staring at the waitress's A-cups. "I like them all. Little ones. Big ones."

She laughed. "Well, we actually do have a special menu for those interested in more than just food." She lowered her voice and nodded toward the stage. "And Bella is our special tonight."

Duke licked his chops. "How much would that run me?"

"Two hundred bucks for a full course… serving," she replied.

He whistled. "Damn, she worth it?"

"Couldn't tell you. I don't swing that way," she said with a wink.

"We'll just take the beers right now," Jordan interrupted, getting irritated. They were there for one thing, and one thing only—Hailey. He needed Duke's full attention.

Taking the hint, the waitress left to get their beers.

"We don't have time for fucking around," Jordan said to Duke. "Not to mention, we don't want to draw any extra attention to ourselves. You know what I'm saying?"

He nodded.

"Once we get back to Farmington, you can take a few hours off and get your willy waxed."

Duke smirked.

The waitress returned with their beers and then left again.

"Hey, is that her?" Duke nodded toward the entrance a few minutes later.

Jordan turned and stared as a long-haired brunette entered the bar. Hailey's natural hair color was blonde, but he expected her to be hiding it. As for her height and body structure, the young woman had a similar frame. Unfortunately, her face was blocked by the oversized sunglasses she wore. Considering they were in a dark club, it was odd she was wearing any at all.

"I don't know. I can't see her face. It could be her," Jordan said. He sniffed the air, trying to find the bitch's scent. Unfortunately, there were too many other smells getting in the way. Not to mention, it was possible Hailey had learned to mask hers.

"What should we do? Follow her?" Duke asked as they watched the woman turn and head down a hallway.

"Not yet. Let's wait for her to come back out so we can get a better look at her."

Duke nodded.

The place started to fill up with more customers while they waited. Meanwhile, strippers moved from table-to-table, flirting and offering lap dances.

"Damn, where is she?" Duke muttered. "All this nakedness is driving me crazy."

Jordan drummed his fingers on the table quickly. He was feeling more and more anxious by the minute. "Maybe she saw us?"

Duke frowned. "Should I go back there and try to find her?"

He looked toward the hallway again, where she'd disappeared.

Was there an EXIT?

Had she slipped out?

If so, she'd be long gone by now.

He frowned. "Not yet. Maybe she's not just waitressing and getting into costume?"

Duke's eyes lit up. "Wouldn't that be something?"

Jordan gave him a dirty look. Best friend, or not, he didn't want anyone else lusting after Hailey. It pissed the hell out of him.

Noticing, Duke changed the subject. "Maybe I should go outside while you keep watch in here? If she does sneak out, I'll see her."

"Good idea."

Duke quickly finished his beer and slipped out the front.

The waitress returned and picked up his empty beer bottle. "Where's your friend?" she asked, looking around.

"He had to make a call. Say, I thought I saw Amy walk in. Is she working tonight?"

"Yeah, she's in back talking with the manager, I think. She should be out shortly. You friends with her?"

"Oh, yeah." Jordan smiled. "We go *way* back."

He could tell the waitress was trying to figure out if that was a good thing or not.

"We're cousins," he added.

She smiled. "Oh, cool. Would you like me to tell her you're here?"

"No. I want it to be a surprise." He took another swig of his beer and set it down. "I'm in town for business and we hardly get to see each other."

"Oh, okay." She nodded toward his beer. "Looks like you're almost empty. Want another?"

"Actually, I'm good." He leaned closer to her. "So… going back to that private menu you spoke about earlier. Is Amy on it?"

The waitress gave him a weird look.

"It's not like that," he said quickly, chuckling. "I just want to surprise her. I think it would be hilarious if I set up a meeting and she walked in to find me there, instead of a customer."

She smiled. "Yeah, I imagine it would."

"How do I sign up?"

Ten minutes later, Jordan sat in one of the private VIP rooms, waiting for good ol' cousin "Amy." He'd already texted Duke, letting him know what was happening. Now, all he had to do was catch her by surprise, use the chloroform in his pocket, sneak her out of the club, and drag her ass back to Farmington. Unless… he lost his shit and murdered the bitch first.

Jordan checked his watch, the anticipation killing him as the seconds ticked by. It didn't take long before the sound of footsteps drew his attention.

As they moved closer, he stood up, ready to grab her if she bolted.

The woman stopped on the other side of the privacy curtain and cleared her throat before pulling it aside.

"Hello there, handsome. I heard you asked for me?" the brunette said with a coy smile.

Jordan stared at her.

Was it Hailey?

He couldn't be sure.

The woman standing there had on Daisy-duke shorts and a black tank top with the *Triple B* logo. Her skin was pale and she was definitely voluptuous, like Hailey. Unfortunately, he couldn't see her eyes, because she still had on the damn sunglasses. He also couldn't catch her natural scent. It was overpowered by the smell of booze, pot, and cheap perfume.

He nodded.

"Let's get this party started then." She stepped into the room, a little wobbly on the four-inch stilettos she wore.

Had that been Hailey's voice?

It seemed husky. Too husky.

Frustrated, he pointed to her sunglasses. "Take those off."

"Now, hold on, cowboy. Business before pleasure," she replied, placing a hand on her hip. "Let's discuss price. What exactly do you want from me?"

Having lost all patience, he reached out and tugged the sunglasses from her face abruptly. Her pupils were dilated and she appeared to be stoned out of her mind. She also wasn't Hailey.

"Hey! What the hell?" she snapped angrily.

Jordan let out a sigh.

Another waste of time.

Glaring at him, the stripper held out her hand. "Give me back my sunglasses. You had no right doing that."

He tossed them at her.

Amy laughed coldly. "Forget this. You're an asshole. I don't need this shit. I'm outta here." She turned around to leave.

Furious that another woman was walking out on him without permission, Jordan grabbed her around the waist and clamped his hand over her mouth. "You don't leave unless I say you do," he growled.

Amy began to kick and thrash around.

Her struggling excited him. His cock was harder than it had been in a long time. Jordan thought about taking her back to the van so they could have some fun with the bitch. But, she wasn't Hailey and he might not hold the erection. He didn't want her ridiculing him in front of Duke. He also didn't want her causing a scene in the club, which she'd do if he let her go.

Fuck.

With one swift motion, he broke her neck and then released her. She crumpled to the floor and stared up at him with dead eyes.

Jordan reached into his back pocket and pulled out his wallet. He opened it up and dropped a hundred dollar bill onto her motionless body. Considering he was still as hard as a rock, he felt she deserved a fat tip.

"I might be an asshole, but I'm not a cheap one," he mused, turning away. As he was about to leave, he caught his reflection in the mirror. Even in his disguise, he looked damn good.

Hailey was indeed an idiot.

Not only was he on his way to becoming the Alpha of his pack, he was one handsome son-of-a-bitch. Some women just didn't know a good thing when they saw it.

1

Briar Lake
Six Months Later

Hailey

"Jillian. He's here," Keri said in a stage whisper. One that was loud enough for the entire diner to hear.

I knew *exactly* who Keri was talking about. And, without turning around, knew *exactly* what he'd be doing—swinging one long, lean leg over the counter stool at my station. It was the same motion he used to climb onto his motorcycle and... sexy as hell.

Next, he'd grab a menu, which was pretty pointless considering he always ordered the exact same thing—coffee. Black.

Finally, he'd run a hand through that thick ebony hair of his and hunch his shoulders while glancing down at the greasy plastic in his hands. Whether he was really reading it or not, it didn't really matter. He never changed his order. It was always the coffee.

A shiver of anticipation ran through me as I thought about his handsome face and intense gaze. Those piercing blue eyes were unnerving. They actually had a physical effect on me. It was almost ...scary.

The first time he hit me with that gaze reminded me of the time I'd gone ass-end over the handlebars of my bike, back when I was ten. I'd landed hard on the pavement, the wind knocked out of me. I'd almost forgotten that feeling until I looked into his eyes for the first time. They were the color of the ocean and just about as deep. When our eyes met, it had felt like everything around us had disappeared. Including the air. Or maybe I'd just forgotten how to breathe.

"Jillian…your man is waiting," reminded Keri in an amused voice.

Pulling myself together, I gave her a dirty look.

Amused, Keri winked, giggled, and flounced her way to the other end of the counter.

Smoothing down my apron, I approached him, reminding myself to get my shit together before he looked up. I was there to make money, not moon after strangers. No matter how hunky they were.

"Hi. Are you ready to order?" I asked, mentally kicking myself as the words left my lips. He'd been coming in since Monday, and I'd said the same thing, *exactly*, five times.

Was it so hard to think of something, anything, other than that?

He looked up and his eyes did their magic—stirring up the butterflies in my stomach. "Coffee, please. Black," he replied. "Shocker, huh?"

I grinned stupidly. "Yes. I mean, no. Uh, you said black?"

He chuckled. "Yeah."

"Okay." Normally, I was great at building tickets. With anyone else, I'd ask if he or she might enjoy a muffin or cinnamon roll with their coffee. Hell, even toast. But, just like before, I couldn't seem to get more than a couple of words out.

I was so pathetic.

"You have something on your cheek," he said, pointing toward his own.

I raised my fingers to my face. Sure enough, I'd been walking around with ketchup on my cheek.

Thanks for nothing, Keri.

I wiped my fingers on my apron. "Ketchup. I, um, I was refilling the bottles. Some were hard to open."

"No worries. I just thought you'd want to know."

"Yes. Thank you."

"No problem."

I slipped my pen and pad back into my apron while making a mental note to volunteer Keri for ketchup duty next shift. Of course, not before I tightened the hell out of them first.

He leaned forward to put the menu back, but it slipped out of the metal holder on the counter. I tried retrieving it and his fingers brushed against mine. What happened next hit me like a tidal wave. Images flashed in my mind of gray and white fur and sharp canines. It was followed by an intense urge to rip off both of our clothes and rub my naked body against his…

What the actual hell?

Trembling, I staggered back. The menu hit the floor with a slap. In shock, all I could do was stare down at it while the blood rushed through me.

"You okay?" he asked, looking startled.

Our eyes met, only this time… I wasn't so clueless. I knew why I'd been reacting so strongly to him.

He was a Lycan.

"I'm fine," I squeaked.

The front door jingled and more customers walked in, startling me out of my daze. Turning, I stumbled away and headed to the back of the diner, where I ran into Keri.

"You okay?" she asked, staring at me with concern. "You look like you've seen a ghost. Wait a second, did it have something to do with hot-stuff back there? Did he say something inappropriate? Sometimes guys that good looking are real assholes."

I forced a smile to my face. "No. He was fine. I'm fine. We both are… fine," I replied nervously. "I'm just… clumsier than usual today. I probably should have gotten more sleep."

"Okay. You had me worried there for a second." Keri lowered her voice and smirked. "Let me guess. He wants just coffee again? Black?"

"Yeah."

"I can tell you like him." Her eyes searched mine. "Maybe you should ask if he'd like a little pie with his coffee?" she added with wicked grin.

"Hah. Funny. And I *don't* like him, so give it a rest."

She didn't look convinced. "Whatever you say."

"By the way, thanks for letting me know I had ketchup on my face," I said dryly.

Her eyebrows shot up. "You did?"

"Yeah. He told me."

Keri's cheeks turned pink. "Seriously, I didn't notice. I lost a contact and can only see out of one eye."

I relaxed. "It's fine. Just a little embarrassing."

"I once had black pepper in my teeth all day and nobody told me. Not just one speck, either. An entire fleet of pepper flakes. I know your pain, girl."

I smiled and hurried over to the coffeepot, my mind returning to the other Lycan. I was almost certain that he had no clue about me. My mother, before she'd died in a car accident, had taught me how to mask everything that might give away my true self. With humans, keeping that secret was a piece of cake. With other shifters, it was a whole different story. But, over the years, I'd gotten pretty damn good at it. I'd stayed hidden and hadn't run into any trouble.

The real question was—*why* wasn't he hiding who he was, and were there others in town?

Of course, it was possible that he was the only shifter in Briar Lake, which was why he didn't bother to mask his scent. I could only hope that was the case.

I stole a glance in his direction. The guy was more questions than answers. The only thing I knew for certain was that he was dangerous and I had to be careful.

I walked back over and poured him a cup of coffee, slopping some of it into the saucer because of my shaky hand.

"Sorry," I said, avoiding his face.

"No problem. You okay?"

I looked up and our eyes met. "Yeah."

His gaze held mine and I wavered between walking away, and drilling him with questions. Now that I knew he was a shifter, my reaction to him made sense. I could now deal with it. What I couldn't figure out was why he'd been coming to the diner every day, sitting in my section, and not doing anything but ordering coffee.

Did he know about me?

Had *I* actually slipped?

I didn't think so. Being a female shifter, one had to be on constant guard. There were fewer of us and I wasn't about to become anyone's bitch. Not to mention, I had to stay hidden for my own safety.

Still, I was dying to know more about him and whether or not he was a threat. I was tired of moving from town-to-town and had gotten comfortable in Briar Lake.

I took a deep breath, ready to ask a few idle questions, the normal kind a waitress might ask a customer, when all hell broke loose.

2

Ransom

Ten Minutes Earlier

"What the hell's wrong with the coffee here? Why do you have to go out to get it?"

I glanced over at my boss, Reece. He sat on the edge of his wooden desk, his heavy brows drawn together as he examined an old Harley carburetor. The desk behind him held an assortment of tools, rags, and other motorcycle parts in various stages of disassembly. I wondered if Reece ever did any work in the shop. Every time I'd gone looking for him, I'd find the guy in his office, tinkering with stuff.

I held up the glass coffee pot, swirling with inky liquid. As usual, the smell of burned coffee, mingled with years of accumulated oil, grease and sweat, permeated throughout the shop "I go out for coffee because… this stuff is shit. We have motor oil that's thinner than this." I set the pot back on the burner.

His eyes narrowed and he shook his head. "You know, Ransom, if you weren't such a good mechanic…"

I grunted. "If I weren't such a good mechanic, what? You'd throw me out?"

He gave me a rueful smile. "Yeah, I know, it would be a waste of time. I'd still be stuck with you. You're family."

"Which is the only reason I put up with your shit," I countered, smirking.

Used to my cocky replies, Reece waved a grease-stained hand in my general direction. "Go, then. Get your fancy swill so you can get your ass back and do some work. We have three new work orders that came in. One of them is for Malone, and I don't want that slacker Grady working on his bike. It will never get done."

Fancy swill?

It honestly wasn't much better than the coffee Reece offered. But, the server seemed to make it taste so much better. "Got it."

I left the shop and strode down the sidewalk. It was a nice day already and only supposed to get better. The mid-morning sun was warm and the breeze carried just a hint of spring flowery scents from the nearby lilac bushes.

I drew a deep breath, wishing that the diner was far enough away to ride my motorcycle. But a half-block didn't warrant taking it out, as much as I wanted to. I'd done it once and had felt foolish. It had taken longer to park the damn thing than it had to ride it over. Knowing there was no rain in sight, I decided I would take it for a spin after work, before the sun set. It would have to do.

Betty's wasn't the only diner within walking distance, and the coffee certainly wasn't the reason I went there each day. Hell, I could have even done without it, but wasn't about to give up my daily fix of the waitress, who worked the breakfast shift. Coffee was just the only excuse I could give Reece for going there.

It all started one day, after arguing about something with Reece. Although we were family, we were always butting heads. Hell, maybe it was *because* we were family. Anyway, that morning I'd needed to leave the shop to calm down and had wandered in to *Betty's* for the hell of it. After taking a spot at the counter, I'd grabbed a menu at had been checking out the specials, when a female voice drew my attention. Looking up from the menu, I'd locked eyes with a woman so gorgeous, I'd had to do a double-take. Blonde hair and curves in the right areas. The kind that belonged in a Sports Illustrated centerfold.

As hot as she was, however, her eyes had taken it up another level. They were gray, a shade bordering on silver, and like nothing I'd seen before. She was the entire package, if not more. For the first time in my life, I'd found myself completely mesmerized. Not to mention, painfully aroused.

"Hi. Are you ready to order?"

"Coffee, please," I'd croaked. "Black."

"Okay."

Then she was off to fetch it and even her back view was worth the price of a crappy cup of coffee. Although her ass had been hidden under the uniform, she had lean, strong calves and hips that swayed provocatively as she walked away.

Coffee, please. Black…

I'd kicked myself for not coming up with something more original on that first day. Or the next few. But, here it was, a week later, and no other words had really been spoken between us. I was way off my game and it was frustrating.

What in the hell was wrong with me?

Women—and motorcycles—were my vice. Having either of them under me was the ultimate thrill. Reece always gave me shit about being a player, and admittedly, I never committed to anyone. But, I wasn't a liar, either. I never promised anything other than a night of fun, maybe two at the most. But this girl, Jillian, according to her nametag, haunted me. She was the first thing I thought about in the morning and the last before falling asleep. My obsession with her was driving me up a wall.

Of course, it was the same today. The breathless anticipation. The buildup, as I watched her work behind the counter. As usual, I felt wound up and couldn't take my eyes off her. I loved the feminine, graceful slant of her neck and the profile of her full lips and high cheekbones. Not to mention she always seemed to be blushing and lowering her long eyelashes after taking my order. She was either really shy or into me as well.

I need to find out...

Enough was enough. I wasn't a young punk. I was a man and needed to act like one. No screwing around.

Determined to walk out of the diner with her number, I sat down in my usual spot and picked up the menu. A few seconds later, she walked over and took my order again.

"Coffee, please. Black." I groaned inwardly after the words left my lips. "Shocker, huh?"

She smiled. "Yes. I mean, no. Uh, you said black?"

I chuckled. "Yeah."

"Okay."

I noticed something on her cheek and told her about it.

"Ketchup. I, um, I was refilling the bottles. Some were hard to open."

"No worries. I just thought you'd want to know." Hell, maybe I shouldn't have said anything. Now she looked embarrassed.

Good going, dumbass.

"Yes. Thank you."

"No problem."

I reached forward to put the menu back, but it slipped out of the metal holder on the counter. She tried helping and our fingers brushed together.

"You okay?" I asked, pulling my hand back quickly, trying to suppress my shock.

She was Lycan.

A shifter.

A young one, but clearly capable of masking herself, and doing a pretty damned good job.

But, not... good enough.

Now I knew why I was so drawn to her. Having been intimate with so many females, mostly human, I was keen on both species, and the waitress was definitely one of my own. Which made me even more aroused.

She'd noticed something, too. I'd seen the shock in her eyes. Not to mention the way she'd left the counter, almost falling in the process. We'd connected in a way that only our kind could, and it had freaked the hell out of her.

"Are you okay?"

"I'm fine," she murmured before taking off.

When she finally made it back with my coffee, I watched her pour it, the silence between us deafening.

"Sorry," she said, spilling a little of it into the saucer.

"No problem."

Our eyes met and I could tell that she was about to say something, when the door jingled and someone walked in.

Jillian looked toward the doorway and her eyes widened in alarm.

Seeing the fear in her face, I turned to look and wondered who the man in the expensive monkey-suit and Ray-Bans was.

3

Hailey

At that instant, it felt as if the world was crashing down on me. The excitement I'd felt a moment before was now replaced with cold-blooded fear. *Jordan.*

He'd finally tracked me down and was there to take me back to the clan—the last thing in the world I wanted.

"Are you okay?"

I was vaguely aware that the guy at the counter was talking to me. I was too focused on the man standing in the doorway.

Jordan took off his sunglasses and shoved them into the pocket of his custom-tailored suit. Armani, no doubt. History told me that his shoes were handmade and probably from the hide of some rare species of animal. Even ruined, they'd be worth more than my car.

With my eyes still locked on Jordan, who hadn't yet noticed me, I sidled down the counter and almost made it to the swinging doors leading to the kitchen. But then, he noticed me.

Our eyes met, and I saw in that instant that he wasn't there to take me back. There was a look of recognition, quickly followed by cold rage. Everything in his expression told me that Jordan wanted to tear me apart, piece-by-piece. It didn't surprise me, however. Not after leaving him at the altar. Not only had I embarrassed him, but Jordan wasn't the kind of guy one walked away from.

My feet suddenly rooted themselves to the floor. Fear wound its numbing fingers around my body as he took a step in my direction.

Run. Get out of here!

But, I couldn't move.

Jordan bellowed my name angrily, his voice cutting through the clatter of the diner. He was going to make a scene, which meant the man was even more irate than I'd imagined.

Shit. Shit. Shit.

Everyone stopped to look at him. In that moment of silence, I could hear my own heartbeat pounding in my ears.

Still pinning me with his eyes, Jordan began moving in my direction, yet all I could do was stare. At the last minute, however, his path was blocked by Coffee Hottie.

"Is there a problem here?" he asked Jordan. The guy's voice was low, controlled, and radiated a power that was a little surprising. It didn't hurt that he had a couple of inches on Jordan.

Jordan glared at him. "That depends. Who the fuck are you?" The edge to his voice was razor-sharp. I recognized by the pitch that he was close to losing his shit, which usually put someone in the hospital or under a gravestone.

"Just a guy trying to keep you from making a mistake that you're going to regret."

Jordan barked out a cruel laugh, then tried to push past him.

Coffee Hottie stopped Jordan with a hand to his chest.

"Take your paw off my shirt, you stinking animal," Jordan growled. "She's mine and I'm not leaving without her."

"Whatever you say." He removed his hand from the shirt, only to grab Jordan's expensive, blood-red silk tie instead. He jerked it hard, pulling Jordan forward. I couldn't actually see the head-butt, but heard the loud crack of bone against bone.

I stared in shock as Jordan collapsed, knocked out from the powerful blow.

"Holy smokes," Keri said, now standing next to me. She looked at Coffee Hottie. "Remind me to never get in your way."

Ignoring her, the stranger looked at me. "Let's go. Before he wakes up."

"Go? We should call the police," Keri said, answering for me.

"I'm the one they'll arrest," the stranger replied and looked my way. "And then who's going to protect you?"

Protect me?

I wasn't an idiot. He was right about everything. I wouldn't make it out of town before Jordan got his paws on me. And… this guy was Lycan. Although I didn't know him, he *had* to be the lesser of two evils.

"You're right," I replied, removing my apron.

"What in the hell is going on?" Keri asked.

"I've gotta go," I said to her. "Don't tell him anything about me."

Keri's eyes widened. "What? You're actually leaving? Who is that guy on the floor? He looked like he was ready to murder you."

"He wanted to." Shivering, I turned around and headed back through the swinging doors into the steamy and chaotic kitchen, with Coffee Hottie following.

"I appreciate what you did back there, but you don't have to protect me," I told him over my shoulder. "I can take care of myself."

"We both know he could have overpowered you in a heartbeat."

"Yeah, but now you've brought trouble upon yourself."

"Do I seem worried?"

Definitely not. In fact, he looked like he'd enjoyed knocking Jordan out.

Glen, the fry cook, gawked as we moved past him. He held a spatula in one hand while his eggs and bacon popped in the greasy pan.

"What's going on out there?" he asked, after spitting out a wad of chew into an empty can.

"You don't want to know. If he comes back here, you never saw me," I said.

His eyebrows shot up. "You're leaving?"

"I have to," I replied.

"Hold up now," he said, not looking happy. "We need you—"

"I know. I'm sorry." I quickly went through the back door, which led to the alley, and blinked in the bright sun. I found myself momentarily disoriented from that and the weight of everything that had occurred. I sagged against the dingy cinderblock wall, wondering how I'd screwed up this time.

How had he found me?

"Who is he to you?" the stranger asked, stepping outside.

I stood up straight. "It's complicated. He's going to try and kill you, you know."

He smirked. "If you haven't noticed, I'm not too worried about that joker."

"You should be. Although, it's not in your DNA is it?"

He raised his eyebrow.

"Male Lycan aren't exactly known for backing down from anything. Even when they should."

"You figured it out?"

"Yeah. When you touched…" I stared down at my hand. "When *we* touched."

"I didn't know about you until then, either."

My ears perked up. I could hear Jordan hollering in the diner. *Damn Lycan healing ability.* Coffee Hottie's head jerked around. He'd heard it, too.

"Dammit, I've wasted too much time. He's conscious," I whispered. "We need to get the hell out of here... uh... what's your name?

"Ransom Hastings. Is your name really Jillian?" He pointed to the nametag, now hanging askew on my uniform. "He called you Hailey."

I glanced down, yanked it off, and pitched it into the dumpster. "That's my real name. Hailey Emerson."

"You usually use an alias?"

"Only when I'm on the run."

There was a crash and a loud yell, which I recognized as Glen's. I quickly moved away from the diner's back door.

"You have a car?" Ransom asked.

Remembering that I'd left my keys and purse under the counter, I swore and told him.

Ransom grabbed my hand and pulled me down the alleyway. He spoke quickly over his shoulder, looking back toward the diner. "You ever been on a motorcycle? I've got mine at the shop, just around the corner."

"Yeah."

We made a headlong dash onto Lindhurst Street, and then he pulled me down another block toward Hearne's Bikes.

"In here," said Ransom.

We burst through the front door, passing a cramped and dusty seating area, to the back of the shop. Ransom then guided me through a welter of bikes in various stages of repair.

"Watch out, Tony," Ransom said to a skinny kid kneeling down next to a bike.

The young man looked up and quickly moved out of our way.

"Ransom? What the hell's going on?" asked a man standing in the doorway to what looked like an office. He held something greasy and metallic in his hand.

"Reece, I'm taking the rest of the day off. Gotta give a girl a ride… somewhere," he replied without breaking his stride.

The older man's jaw dropped. "Excuse me?"

"Sorry, Reece. I'll call you," he said as we headed away.

"Dammit, Ransom!" he hollered. "We don't have time for this shit."

He ignored him. "Bike's out back."

We slammed through a metal security door and popped back out into the bright sunshine. That was when I saw the bike—a big black and silver Harley.

Ransom finally let go of me and I watched as he pulled back the chain-link security gate at the mouth of the alley. A shiver went down my spine as I half expected Jordan to rush us, now that the gate was open.

Reece stepped outside, this time looking more worried than anything. "You need to tell me what's going on."

"I will. Later," Ransom said, wheeling the Harley forward.

Grumbling and shaking his head, the older man walked back into the shop.

Seconds later, the bike came to life with a deep rumble. One that lifted my spirits. It was loud, powerful, and sounded a lot like "escape."

"Come on!" Ransom shouted over the noise of the big machine.

I hiked up the skirt of my waitress uniform and got on behind him.

"Where to?" he asked.

I leaned forward against his broad, muscular back, my lips close to his ear. "My apartment, for a start. Then…" I shrugged and leaned back. "I guess I'll figure things out from there."

"Where's your apartment?"

I told him. "You know that area?"

"Yeah." He gunned the big machine, dropped it into gear, and then we were off.

4

Ransom

As we drove through the streets toward her place, I thought back to the incident in the diner. I'd known the guy was Lycan the moment the door opened and he'd stepped inside. His scent had been so strong, rolling off of him in waves. I figured the guy was either supremely egotistical, thinking it would deter other shifters from messing with him. Or, he was so out of control that he didn't even think to mask himself.

As it turned out, he was both.

I'd been close to a few loose cannons in my life and he definitely fell into that category. Something told me that this guy was beyond anything I'd ever encountered, too. A real nut-job with a God-complex. For a brief second, I'd even debated about getting involved. But, the look on the girl's face had gotten to me and there'd been no way I could just sit there and let whatever happen, happen. For one thing, she was clearly terrified of him. For another, I had a feeling that if she ran, I'd never see her again. And, I couldn't let that happen either.

So, I'd stood and turned to face the guy, only to bite back a laugh. The shifter had barely made it to my chin, and looked like he spent a small fortune on clothing. Maybe trying to make up for the lack of stature—or lack of something else—with the flashy clothes?

As far as I was concerned, neither mattered. All that was important now was keeping myself between the guy and the girl. I wasn't sure what she'd done to fuel his rage, but it had radiated off of him like a damn furnace. The shifter was definitely out for more than just claiming the female as his own.

He wanted her blood.

When I'd put my hand on his shirt, I'd caught myself a glimpse of just how wound up he'd been. Hell, it wouldn't have surprised me if the guy had shifted into his Lycan form right then and there. In broad daylight.

"Take your paw off my shirt, you stinking animal. She's mine and I'm not leaving without her."

I'd reacted, instinct and intense dislike for the guy fueling my actions. Grabbing his tie, I'd yanked hard and slammed my forehead into his face. I'd perfected the move over the years, knowing just when and how hard to do it. There'd been a satisfying crack when my head connected with the bridge of the guy's nose. Thankfully, he'd blacked out, providing enough time to put some distance between them.

And now Jillian—or Hailey, as it turned out—was on the back of my bike as we weaved through lunch-hour traffic. While we burned through a multitude of yellow lights, it was pretty clear she'd been on a bike before. She moved with me around the corners, thankfully not clutching my waist in a death-grip like some women did. Especially going as fast as we were.

Despite our speed, and the cars honking, not all of my focus was on the road or the maniac we were running from. My horny self was acutely aware of her arms hugging me. The soft press of her breasts against my back. Not to mention those warm hands on my stomach, just above the button of my jeans. And, when she'd hiked up her skirt to climb on behind me, I'd caught a flash of long legs and creamy thighs. It had caused several wicked thoughts to run through my head.

With my mind on other things, a large, yellow taxi pulled up in front of me, forcing me to react.

Fuck.

Braking wasn't an option, so I gunned the machine and leaned hard, swerving around the ass-end of the cab. I drew a deep breath as we rocketed through the other side of the intersection safely. Sighing in relief upon clearing it, I tore my mind away from Hailey's attributes so as not to get us killed.

"You okay?" I called out.

"Yeah. You remember which street?"

"Yep."

She'd shouted it in my ear, back when we'd been traveling under the speed limit. Fortunately, I knew the area and it wasn't long before we were cruising down Belmont Street, past the red brick apartment buildings, which had seen not only better days, but better decades. Soon, I felt her hand move away from my waist before pointing to one of the cookie cutter buildings.

"Okay," I replied loudly.

I noticed an alley and turned down the shadowy canyon running between her building and its neighbor. From there, we entered a courtyard, where a multitude of weeds grew with abandon. I swung into it, making a tight circle across the patchy, brown grass before coming to a complete stop. Hailey was off the bike before I had a chance to kill the engine.

I kicked the stand down and got off the bike, watching as she raced up a set of cracked, cement steps.
With one last glance at my Hog, I followed her through a back door and into a dim hallway, which smelled like cat urine and cooked cabbage.

"Do you think this is a good idea? What if he knows where you live?" I asked, trying not to breathe in the foul scent.

She fumbled with her keys in front of a nondescript door. The number eight was missing from it, but the ghostly outline was still visible on the dingy wood. Hailey hesitated and then shoved the key into the lock. "We'd probably know by now—the door would probably be kicked in. Anyway, I just need to get my stuff and grab some money. It won't take long."

"Okay."

We walked in and she slammed the door shut behind us, throwing the deadbolts. She turned back around to face me, looking anxious.

"Stay here," she said. "I'll be right back."

I nodded.

Hailey darted through a pair of curtains into, what I imagined, was her bedroom. I heard banging and thumps and sighed. No woman I'd ever known could organize and pack their shit in less than an hour. Not without some nagging.

"So, you want some help?" I asked, parting the curtains and stepping between them. The first thing I noticed was the secondhand furniture and clothing strewn around everywhere. Then I saw Hailey and stopped dead in my tracks. She stood in the middle of the room, in just her bra and panties, glaring at me.

"What the hell? I'm getting dressed here."

"Sorry. I just wanted to see if I could help," I stammered, unable to take my eyes off her round curves. I knew it was rude to stare, but I couldn't seem to pull my gaze away.

Noticing, she grabbed a small blanket from the bed and pulled it against her to cover up. "I'm packed. Turn around, damn it, so I can finish getting dressed."

I turned my back, but the image of Hailey was engraved in my mind. The body I'd imagined, beneath her waitress uniform, was a far cry from what I'd gotten a good look at. It was pretty clear, even in the dim light from the cloudy window, that I'd underestimated just how beautiful she was.

"So, you're already packed? That must be a new record somewhere," I said, hearing the rustle of clothing behind me.

Hailey cleared her throat. "You, uh, you ever heard of a *bug-out* bag? The preppers have them. Well, so do I."

"Preppers?" I frowned, trying to gauge where she was with getting dressed. Damn if I didn't want another glimpse of her. Realizing how much of an asshole that made me, I mentally kicked myself. The girl was obviously in danger and all I could think about was what she looked like in her bra and panties.

"Yeah, you know? 'End-of-the-world' people. Doomsday preppers. The survivalists. You can turn around."

I did and found that she was dressed in jeans and a T-shirt.

Hailey sat down on the edge of her bed and began pulling on a pair of Doc Martens. "Anyway, a *bug-out* bag has all of your essentials for survival. For a few days, at least. Mine's a little different, since it has pretty much everything I own." She nodded to the duffel on the floor at the foot of her bed. Of course, I hadn't even noticed it. My mind had been on other things.

"So, this guy's been after you for a while then?" I asked, curious about their relationship.

Hailey stood, yanked the binder from her hair, setting it free. Blonde curls cascaded over her shoulders. I watched as she pulled it all back again, securing it behind her head.

"Three-and-a-half years. I've been in this town for…" She scowled, bent, and hoisted the duffel onto her shoulder. "Something like four months. Dammit, I really thought I'd lost him this time."

"He must be pretty relentless."

"Oh, yeah." Hailey shouldered past me, heading for the compact living room. She dropped the duffel and I watched as she yanked aside a corner of the floor rug. She dropped to her knees and proceeded to pull up one of the floorboards.

"Need any help?" I asked, moving closer.

"No. I got it." Reaching between the joists, she pulled up a leather satchel. "Just need to make a withdrawal from the bank."

"Smart. Keeping it here and hidden," I replied, wondering how much she had stored away.

"Yeah, well, I've learned my lesson. Let me tell you." She stood in front of me, her face slightly flushed. "Look, I apologize for dragging you into this, but I've got to get the hell out of here. Jordan's going to pick up my trail pretty soon, or he's going to beat my address out of someone at the diner, if he hasn't already. Anyway, thanks for the ride," she said, sounding winded. Hailey hoisted the duffel, slung the strap over her shoulder, and grabbed the satchel of cash.

Panic surged through me. She was headed out the door, and if I let her go… she'd be out of my life.

In the few seconds that it took her to reach the other side of the room, I'd made up my mind. "Wait. You can't go back to the diner for your car. He'll find you. I'll take you wherever you want to go."

She turned, eyes wide. "You'd do that? Just up and leave town with me?"

I nodded.

Her face became guarded and she frowned. "Why the hell would you do that? You don't even know me."

"True." I took a step toward her. "But if I let you go now, I'll never get the chance to get to know you. And…"

I moved closer and her scent washed over me. First, the sharp tang of fear and anxiety, the most obvious. Beneath that were flowers and spice and… something deeply feminine. Something overwhelmingly like home. "…I'm not willing to pass up that chance."

She looked up at me and blinked. Then her face flushed a pretty pink. Her lips parted. "Oh. Well…I…"

I bit back a smile. She *was* interested in me and not just because I offered a way out. "Just tell me one thing, though."

Hailey took a deep breath, then nodded. "Okay."

"Who's the guy, and why's he chasing you?"

"That's two things…" Hailey smiled and I noticed she had dimples and a light splash of freckles across her cheeks.

How had I missed those?

She looked me dead in the eyes. "He's the son of my clan's Alpha."

No surprise there. Especially with that arrogance of his.

"Why's he chasing you?"

Hailey hesitated, but her eyes never left mine. I waited until she dropped the bomb.

"I left him at the altar."

5

Hailey

"Hell, when you decide to piss someone off, you really go all out, don't you?" Ransom said with a smirk. "His father must not be too happy with you, either."

I shifted under the weight of the duffel and Ransom's intense scrutiny. Personal history wasn't something I liked talking about. I certainly hadn't ever told anyone about Jordan, or being a runaway bride. Keri and Glen, from the diner, knew me as a good Irish girl from the other side of town. A part-time college student trying to earn a Liberal Arts degree. Before that, in an entirely different state, I'd been Lisbeth, working at a preschool and teaching kids to draw. I'd told people there I was paying off student loans, after dropping out of art school. Before that…I didn't really remember. The lies seemed to be never-ending, as did running away and starting over. I was exhausted mentally and physically.

I shifted the duffel again. "Let's just say that it's not a good situation, any way you look at it."

This was hard. Everything inside of me screamed that it was insanity to trust a stranger, especially a male Lycan. For all I knew, Jordan could have sent him to track me down. Except… the head-butt at the diner sort of ruled that out. Still, I really knew nothing about him, only that he'd been a life-saver up to this point. Now he was offering to get me out of town, which gave me a tiny sprout of hope for the future. That, and the feeling I might not have to do this by myself anymore, eased me a bit. It was enough, at least for now.

"Anyway, you said you'd take me out of here?"

His blue eyes felt like lasers burning into mine. Intense and probing. "I did. Just tell me where."

I chuckled dryly. "Well, about that…"

He waited.

I looked toward the doorway. I needed to make a decision. Trust a stranger with my life, or go back outside, alone. "The thing is… I don't really have any place to go."

That was the truth. I'd run before, but each time I'd had more warning. A type of sixth-sense telling me that Jordan was hot on my trail. Sometimes the hair on the back of my neck would go up, or there'd be the familiar sense of being watched. The alarm bells would sound off in my head and I knew to get out of town, no questions asked. I'd always listened to those feelings and knew it was what kept me two steps ahead of Jordan. This time, there'd been nothing.

It was unsettling.

Of course, it was possible that I'd just gotten careless somehow. Had moved too close to home. Slipped up with the name I'd chosen or the job I was currently at. Or, maybe it was just that Jordan had gotten better at tracking me down. He had a powerful clan, with an influential Alpha backing him, while I was out in the cold, all alone.

Ransom was quiet and I began to wonder if I'd blown it. That maybe this was much more than he wanted to handle. Playing the hero once, and dragging me out of danger's way, might be his limit for the day. I couldn't exactly blame him either. We were strangers and he didn't owe me anything. Not to mention, I wasn't an idiot. I knew he wanted me, but the price was going up for him by the minute.

"Nowhere, huh?" he said, biting his lower lip. "Shit."

And there it was. My answer.

I sighed, turned the doorknob, and stepped into the hall, dreading what might be waiting for me outside. "Don't worry about it," I said, feeling disappointed, although I really didn't have any right to be. He'd done so much already. "I'll figure something out."

"Hey."

I turned to look at him.

"I know of a place."

A couple hours later, we were once again on his motorcycle, charging down some backwoods road, far away from the city. Ransom had mentioned he knew of a place, but I'd assumed it was somewhere in the civilized world. Apparently, that wasn't going to be the case.

I closed my eyes. We'd been riding at breakneck speeds, going up and down small green hills, for the most part. Recently, however, the bike had started climbing what felt like a completely vertical sloped terrain, followed by descents that had my stomach in my throat.

I shivered.

The air was cool, almost cold. I needed my jacket, but didn't want to ask Ransom to stop. For one thing, I thought we'd made good time; the more distance between me and Jordan, the better. But more to the point, there didn't seem to be any place where we actually could stop. The road was narrow and lined with trees. Although we were in the middle of nowhere, traffic was still pretty heavy, too. Especially with the abundance of semis traveling from city to city. I decided to tough it out and let him decide when and where we'd stop.

It was almost dark when Ransom finally turned down a gravel road. We drove on for several minutes and then eventually, he slowed and swung the bike toward the edge of the road.

What the hell was he doing?

There wasn't anything in sight. We were totally alone and my paranoia was rearing its ugly head.

Had I made a mistake?

It was almost too much of a coincidence that Jordan had walked into the diner just a few days after Ransom.

But then I saw another gravelly roadway, this one almost hidden by the trees in the splashing light of the bike, and relaxed.

Ransom followed the trail, which wound down, and then back up, beneath the canopy of pines. After about another mile, he stopped in a small clearing and cut the engine.

"We're almost there," he told me. "We need to walk the rest of the way, though."

"Okay."

I climbed off and staggered slightly as my legs became accustomed to walking on solid ground again.

Ransom followed suit and began stretching out. I watched, fascinated by the way his hard muscles rippled beneath the black T-shirt as he moved and flexed. Here, I'd just been tracked down by an ex-almost-husband, dragged to safety by a total stranger, even fleeing the city with him. Now, all I could think about was how sexy Ransom looked, which was crazy, but something I just couldn't help.

Perfect timing to start drooling over someone, I thought wryly.

Sure, I had hit it off with other guys, but I had to admit that the chemistry between Ransom and me was undeniable. Riding behind him for hours hadn't hurt…or helped.

I'd pretty much already mapped out the contours of his muscular stomach under the guise of adjusting my hold on his waist while on the back of his bike. The way his shoulders moved, or the feel of his muscles tensing, relaxing, and shifting beneath my cheek, had become familiar and comforting. All of it—aided by the vibration of the big machine beneath me—had also awakened something long dormant inside.

"So… where's here and where's almost?" I asked, trying to get my head straight.

"We're close to Clyde, and 'almost' is a cabin."

I raised my eyebrow. "Who's Clyde?"

Ransom undid the straps holding my duffel and I grabbed it off the back of the bike. Of course, I still carried the satchel, the long strap slung across my body. No way would I trust that to a bungee cord on the back of a bike. Clothes, shoes, even the toothbrush… all I could do without. But the stuff in the satchel was irreplaceable.

"Not a 'who'. A 'where'. It's a little town in North Carolina, and we're outside of it by about twenty miles," he replied.

"Oh."

He did what was needed to secure his bike and then unpacked a small, black backpack. He hung the strap over his shoulder and motioned toward the trees.

"It's this way, just a short hike through the woods. The path is well-marked. Should be pretty easy for you in those boots," Ransom said.

"Good. Lead the way."

He turned and I followed, pushing aside brush and tree limbs. If there was a path, I really had no idea where it was hiding. Ransom seemed to be carving it out as we went.

"Are you sure you know where you're going?" I asked before a branch slapped my face and a bramble wound its thorny fingers around my ankle. I quickly leaned down and removed it while he disappeared ahead of me.

"Yeah. Been coming here on and off since I was a kid," he said from somewhere up ahead.

"Crap," I mumbled, standing back up. The last thing I needed was to get lost in unfamiliar territory.

I scanned the dark forest, trying to get a line on Ransom. Everything smelled like pine and cold air. "Hey, can you wait? I'm stuck…" I yanked at another vine and impaled myself on something sharp, causing me to yelp in pain.

"You okay?" His voice was so close it startled me.

Amazed at how he'd appeared so quickly, I waved my hand toward the prickly vines. "Yeah. I'm just…" I smiled weakly. "Having problems, I guess."

"Here…" Ransom took my hand, guiding me back to what I guessed was the path. At least it didn't have things that lunged out, trying to kill me. After getting me back on course, he pulled his hand away.

"You're not much of a nature girl, are you?" he asked, moving slower so I could keep up this time.

"Not so much. The most I've ever experienced was an overgrown backyard as a kid."

He gave me a surprised look. "You've never tracked?"

"I've never had to track anyone through the forest. Through the city, now *that's* a different story. Nothing can hide from me there."

"The wilderness is where it's at. You don't have to hide who you really are. Plus, you can be at one with nature. If I had it my way, I'd spend all of my time out here."

"You wouldn't get bored?"

"I'd find things to keep me busy," he replied with a twinkle in his eyes. Suddenly, his eyes hardened and he looked distracted.

"What is it?"

"Not sure. The cabin's just ahead, though." His voice was low, just above a growl.

A sour wave of fear rushed through me.

Could Jordan have found us already?

I knew it was a longshot, but I didn't put anything past him. I couldn't afford to.

Anxious, I tried sniffing the air, but didn't notice anything alarming. This wasn't my territory, however. Thank goodness he knew what he was doing.

"Anything?" I whispered, watching his nose twitch.

"No. It's okay."

I sighed in relief.

Ransom stepped forward, his body relaxing. "There's a trail up ahead, not far down the hill. Sometimes hikers get lost and end up here. Might have been what I smelled."

Learning that he'd actually caught someone's scent made the hair stand up on the back of my neck. "You're sure? It's not…"

He gave me a reassuring look. "No. It's human, not shifter. And days old."

I sighed in relief. His senses were much more advanced than mine, thankfully.

We walked down a short path, through another open clearing, until we reached a small cabin. Its outline was barely visible against the night sky. As we drew closer, I could now smell what must have alerted Ransom. It was the faintest of human scent.

"Wait here," he told me.

I nodded.

He walked up to the cabin and I heard metal on metal, followed by the creak of a door opening. He stepped inside and a few seconds later, yellow light spilled down the path, momentarily blinding me.

"Everything is clear. Come on up," he called through the darkness.

I climbed the short flight of wooden steps and moved past him in the doorway. "How do you get electricity up here?" I asked, stepping inside.

"I have two generators. Thankfully, they haven't been stolen."

"Ah."

The cabin was small, clean, and extremely organized. I headed into the kitchen, which was also uncluttered and appeared to have everything one might need. There was even an empty flower vase.

"So, is this *your* cabin?" I asked, setting my duffel on the floor.

"It's been in the family for a few generations. My great grandfather grew up in the area. He built this and lived here 'til he died. It was passed down from father to son, until… me."

"And you're the last of the line?" I wondered about the man, back at the bike shop. Was he a shifter, too? Something told me they were pretty close. Maybe even family.

Ransom glanced up, giving me a rueful smile. "Yeah, sort of. I guess I'm what you'd call a loner. Kind of funny, considering how much we're supposed to be clan animals."

I walked to the other side of the cabin, to a big window, and peered outside. I imagined that during the day it looked out over a meadow. Right now, the dark glass reflected back my own image. Tangled hair. Drawn Face. Anxiety.

I turned around and smiled gratefully. "Thanks for…well, thanks for this,"

"No problem."

A simple "thank-you" almost felt inadequate. Ransom had done far more than just give me a roof for the night.

I swallowed and walked toward him. "I mean, you're risking so much for me. A total stranger. Not only did you help me escape Jordan, but you're putting yourself in so much danger now by hiding me."

"It was the right thing to do. Under the circumstances," he said, opening up some of the cupboards.

I thought about Keri and Glen and prayed that Jordan hadn't harmed them. Although I barely knew the two, I felt almost guilty for taking off so quickly and leaving them at his mercy. It made me wonder if I'd actually done the right thing, under the circumstances. I told Ransom my thoughts.

"Don't feel guilty. You had to get out of there. Jordan was out for blood. *Yours.* Anyway, there were other customers coming into the diner as we were leaving. I'm sure Keri and Glen are fine."

"I hope so."

Ransom pulled out some cans of food and set them on the counter. He turned to look at me again. "You hungry? I'm not the best in the kitchen, but I can probably put something together with what we have."

"Yeah, anything is fine, warm or not. I'm starving."

"Okay."

"Do you have a bathroom?"

He tipped his head toward another door, which was down a short hallway. "That way. There are towels inside, so feel free to make yourself at home."

"Thank you. I'm a little…windblown. I could probably use a shower, too."

He gave me a teasing grin. "Yeah, I was going to say…"

I stared at him open-mouthed.

Ransom threw his head back and laughed. "I'm just kidding. You actually smell very nice. Seriously. You always do."

My cheeks grew warm.

I always did?

He's a male Lycan, I reminded myself. *I could shift and roll around in deer dung and he'd still be attracted.*

"Well, under the circumstances, I'll take that as a compliment," I replied.

"Good, because I would never insult you. Not on purpose."

Smiling, I grabbed my duffel bag and headed to the bathroom, the noises in the kitchen following me inside. I closed the door and cringed after a glance in the mirror. My hair was a tangled mess and my face was covered in a layer of road dust. Not to mention… he was actually right. I smelled of sweat…and fear. Not the most alluring of scents.

Despite the small size, the bathroom had a large shower. I turned on the water and was pleasantly surprised that it grew hot pretty quickly. Knowing that it probably wasn't going to last, I stripped out of my clothes and was under the water in seconds. I closed my eyes and sighed in pleasure as it sprayed through my hair and over my shoulders. Turning around, I noticed a bottle of generic shampoo and a bottle of body-wash, resting on the bathtub ledge. As dirty as I was, I used lavish amounts of both.

Overcompensating, I thought, trying too hard to wash away the residue of Jordan more than just the dust and grime from the road.

Before completely using all of the hot water, I reluctantly turned it off. I then dried off with a towel and put on a fresh set of clothes from my duffel.

There wasn't much I could do with my hair, so I settled for a quick comb, leaving it hang down my back. I knew it would soon revolt, rising up in a curly mess. But, life on the run meant unruly hair, which I was pretty used to, anyway.

I walked out of the bathroom and set my duffel bag in the corner.

Noticing me, Ransom pointed to the table. "You're just in time. Have a seat. This is the best I could do under the circumstances."

I sat down and he set a plate in front of me. I looked up at him in amazement. "Spaghetti?"

He nodded.

"Wow, it looks…and smells amazing." I picked up a fork, took a tentative bite, and then dug in with serious intent. "Incredible… what's in it?" I took another mouthful before he could answer.

Ransom sat across from me. "Tomato sauce. I didn't have any meat, so I used some spices from the cupboard to give it more flavor. I also added garlic and onion powder."

"It's so good." I took another mouthful, closing my eyes as I chewed. Either I was starving or it really was the best spaghetti sauce I'd ever had. I figured that it was a little of both. I wasn't much of a cook and most of my meals consisted of frozen dinners or quick meals at the diner.

"Thanks."

Opening my eyes, I caught the smile on his face. He looked quite amused by my enthusiasm over the food.

"How is it that you have running water?" I asked.

"We get it from the well."

"Oh, that makes sense. You really have everything you need out here, don't you?"

"Pretty much. So, are you feeling better?"

"Yes. A lot. Thank you."

"You're welcome."

6

Hailey

Although I had other questions I was dying to ask him, we ate in silence. I could tell he had things on his mind and was quickly learning that he wasn't the most talkative. Neither was I, though, for that matter. Finally, I pushed my plate away and sat back, my hunger satisfied.

I leaned against the chair and thanked him again for dinner.

"It was my pleasure." He took the last bite of his spaghetti and then stood up. I watched as he started clearing the table.

I got out of my chair and picked up my plate. "Let me help you."

We brought the dishes into the kitchen and rinsed them out in the sink. Afterward, Ransom opened up the refrigerator and turned back to me. "I can't believe it. I forgot we had some wine. I'd brought a couple of bottles with me the last time I stopped by. Would you like a glass?"

"Yes. It sounds great. Do you come up here a lot?"

"Whenever I can. I usually come up here a couple weekends a month."

"Nice." I watched him take the wine out of the refrigerator. "I'm a little surprised. I haven't met a lot of guys who drink wine."

"I was raised by wine drinkers. Plus, I have a sweet tooth. Hope you enjoy Moscato?"

"I'm sure I will."

"Make yourself at home," he told me, pulling a corkscrew out of a drawer.

"Okay."

The cabin was small and there wasn't much for furniture. In fact, the only other real option for sitting down, was the bed. As inviting as it looked—and the promises it held—I wasn't ready yet for that, so I sat back down at the table.

As I waited, the low-level hum began in my head again. The subtle noise I'd noticed at the diner seemed like an eternity ago. The pit of my stomach fluttered as I watched him in the kitchen, his back to me. I remembered the warmth of his stomach under my fingers and how erotic it felt, pressing against him on the bike. We weren't on the motorcycle now, and there wasn't anything between us except the old pine table.

Ransom set both glasses of wine on the table and settled back in the chair across from me. The chilled wine was pink and I took a large swallow.

"This is good," I told him.

"Thanks."

I looked around. "You have a really well-stocked kitchen here. In the middle of nowhere. I wasn't expecting anything like this."

Ransom shrugged. "It's my home-away-from-home and I enjoy the solitude. Anyway, with every trip, I try to bring something. Just in case."

"In case of a visitor?"

"I don't get many of those. I do it just in case I suddenly crave something that isn't available to me," he said, his eyes sparkling in the dim light.

The way he was looking at me gave me goosebumps. Now I was also at the cabin. I wondered if he was craving something else entirely, now. He didn't seem like the type to make a bold move, however. And, honestly, I wasn't sure if us having sex was even a good idea.

We sat for many minutes in silence, enjoying the wine. I found Ransom's eyes on me every time I looked up. And that was happening more and more frequently. I noticed more than just his physical interest in me in those blue depths, however. He had questions. I wasn't sure I wanted to start that conversation, so I waited. Of course, it didn't take long for him to ask.

"So, you left the guy at the altar? Did you just get cold feet and bail?"

I sighed. "He's a pretty angry guy, and I…" My voice faltered, as the memory came back. The pain and humiliation I'd felt. The fight or flight response kicking in.

"You ran?"

"I had to. I just couldn't go through with it."

I stopped and he waited patiently for me to tell him more.

I leaned back in my chair and stared ahead, remembering the dark times. "Jordan has always been self-deserving, egotistical, and demanding. But, as time went on, he seemed to get worse. In fact, he'd go into rages where it was like anger blinded him to everything." I stared into space, remembering the physical abuse from Jordan. "He was so aggressive and violent. I hadn't met anyone like him before."

Ransom's eyes hardened. "He beat you? Why?"

I let out a weary sigh. "Because he could."

His eyes searched mine. "Did you fight back?"

I remembered the time he'd almost killed me. It was *because* I'd fought back. "Once. It almost cost me my life. My standing up to him seemed to fuel his fire and," I laughed coldly, "make him stronger, if that's even possible."

"So, you took it."

"Don't get me wrong, I defended myself as much as I could, but I never struck him again. Not after… he almost killed me."

Ransom sighed. "Why did you agree to marry him?"

"I accepted because I didn't think I had a choice. It was expected of me."

"Everyone has a choice."

"Easy for you to say," I mumbled. "You have no idea what it was like living under our Alpha. *His* father."

"You're right. I'm sorry."

I relaxed.

"Tell me more about your clan." Ransom leaned back, and grabbed the wine bottle from the counter. He refilled my glass and then his.

I took another swallow before answering.

"Jordan is the only legitimate son of our Alpha. And, he is one of the most influential men I know. He had connections here, and back in the Old Country. Deep connections. This isn't some New World clan. It goes back… way back."

"Was this an arranged marriage?"

I didn't want to tell him, but he deserved to know everything. I owed him that much. Humiliated by what I was about to confess, I dropped my eyes. "I was payment for a family debt."

Ransom sputtered on his wine. "Really? What the hell kind of family pays their debts with an arranged marriage?"

I shrugged. "Mine. Old family. Old country. Old debt. My father…I guess you could say… *worked* for Jordan's. Apparently, doing unsavory things that nobody else would."

"Like what?"

"I'm not sure, exactly. Something pretty bad, I think. But, I don't know the details. Jordan's father, Travis, offered mine the deal a long time ago. Back when I was still a teenager. I guess that's when whatever happened,

happened. And the bastard took it, rather than be kicked out of the clan."

"So, clan honor wins out over family? That's harsh."

I fidgeted with the wineglass. "My father's old-fashioned. 'Honor the Alpha' above everything," I said dryly.

"He's okay with you being on the run now?"

And this was the hard part, one of many. "My father is dead."

Ransom looked suitably stunned for a moment. "I'm guessing it wasn't old age?"

I shook my head. "Travis had him killed."

His eyes widened. "Why?"

I shrugged. "As a warning, I guess. I found out about it, not long after I ran away. When I was stupid enough to keep in touch with family. I think that's basically how Jordan almost caught up with me the first time. Through my family."

"Killing your father was going to get you to come back to the fold? Kind of seems like overkill… sorry, bad choice of words."

"I don't know if that's the reason why my father was killed. I think my running away was it, but I don't know for sure. It might just be his way of threatening me, or the rest of my family, to obey his wishes."

"And how are you with that? You don't seem too upset…" Ransom's eyes held mine, his forehead furrowed.

"I…well…" I looked down at my hands.

How did I feel?

Good question. I wasn't even sure myself.

"I think 'confused' would probably sum it up in a nutshell. I mean, he sold me to Travis. I hated him for a long time because of that. But then, he was still my father and there were some good memories. Back when I was very young. Anyway, some days I try not to think about it too much."

"So, you've made some dangerous enemies by really pissing Jordan off, it sounds like."

I closed my eyes, rubbing one hand across them. "I know. It's that honor thing. I humiliated Jordan, and when his pride is hurt, he's even more irrational than usual. Of course, Travis backs him. He's the only son. The 'heir' to the throne." I snorted. "A spoiled brat, actually."

"It sounds like it. Still, you'd think he'd just move on instead of killing your old man or going after you."

"I know. Murder seems like a pretty drastic measure. You'd think he'd just be happy that I've tried so hard to drop off the face of the earth. It all doesn't make a whole lot of sense. But when it involves Jordan…he's never been predictable."

Ransom tipped back in his chair. "Well, hell. You are in a tough spot."

I nodded. "Which is why I'm always on the move."

We lapsed back into silence, but my mind spun on. Any rational guy, Lycan or not, wouldn't want this kind of mess in his life. If Ransom took me back to the road now, and left me standing by the side of it, I wouldn't blame him.

Ransom finally sat forward, a serious expression on his face. "Okay… well, we need to figure out a plan. What do you want to do?"

I set my empty glass on the table. "Honestly, I hadn't thought hard about it yet. I just wanted to get away," I smiled sadly. "Planning isn't my specialty. I only know how to run."

"That's just it. You can't keep running, Hailey. It's only a matter of time before he finds you in some place where you can't get away."

I twirled the wine-glass between my fingers, avoiding Ransom's eyes.

He got up from the table and took my empty glass.

"I know…but…" I didn't want to think about it now. My head was fuzzy, partly from the wine, but mostly from thinking about Jordan and Travis.

"I'm going to grab a shower. It's late. If you want to get changed for bed…"

I imagined him in the shower. Water streaming over his muscular, sexy body. I pictured myself, joining him, and my pulse began to race.

As if reading my mind, his own eyes filled with desire. He pushed away from the counter and walked toward me, his eyes locked on mine. The air between us practically crackled, and breathing suddenly became difficult.

"You feel it too, don't you?" he murmured. "This thing between us?"

I nodded.

His hand was suddenly on my arm, sliding up to my neck, cradling the back of my head with strong fingers. I closed my eyes, leaned into his hand, and gave a breathless sigh.

"Hailey…" he said huskily.

The sound of his voice was like sex to my ears. A deep thud hit me. Low. Somewhere south of my bellybutton and north of my knees. Melting everything in between.

I looked at him.

His eyes burned into mine. "It's hard being a gentleman right now."

"Who said you have to be?" I replied softly, surprising myself.

Ransom smiled slowly. "Hold that thought. I'm going to take a shower."

"Okay."

He licked his lips and stared at mine. Just when I thought he might kiss me, Ransom turned around and went into the bathroom.

7

Hailey

I stood for a moment, listening to the shower running. I'd seen it in his eyes, how much he wanted me. The feeling was mutual. Not to mention… intense. Undeniable. Almost… overwhelming. But after everything, it felt right.

A search through my duffel bag turned up nothing remotely sexy. In packing for "life on the run", alluring and sexy hadn't figured into any of my choices. Frustrated, I decided to check the only closet in the cabin, and unearthed a black T-shirt. I assumed it belonged to Ransom and pulled it off of the hanger.

Stripping off everything but my panties, I dragged the T-shirt over my head and then ran my fingers through my hair, which was still slightly damp. Afterward, I walked over and stood by the big window. I looked out over the darkness, rubbing my arms with my hands. A full moon had risen, outlining the trees on the ridge, casting them in black against an indigo sky. It was beautiful.

The sound of the shower stopped and after a moment, the bathroom door opened. In the reflection of the window, I saw the room behind me. I watched as a slice of yellow light cut across the floor. Ransom walked into that slice, naked, and my heart skipped a beat. His body was just as spectacular as I'd sat imagining it would be during the hours on the bike today.

Red-hot desire washed through me in waves. Breathless with anticipation, I watched as he came up behind me and slid his arms around my waist.

"Nice view," I said as we stared out into the darkness.

"Outside? Yeah, it's nice. Inside…" He dropped his head, his breath warm on my neck. "It's spectacular."

Trembling, I closed my eyes.

His hands grabbed the edge of the T-shirt, followed by his fingers brushing against the tops of my thighs. The butterflies that had gathered in my stomach took off. He murmured something against my neck as his lips trailed across my skin and his hands moved higher. He pulled the fabric up, exposing my breasts, and began kneading them with hands, which were still warm and slightly damp from the shower. He pressed against me from behind, molding me against his muscular chest as his hands explored. Down below, I felt his excitement pressing against me and it made my sex clench with hot desire.

"You're so beautiful," he whispered.

I closed my eyes as one hand began a slow return trip back down my stomach, slipping beneath the elastic of my panties. His hands were doing some fairly interesting things to my body and my hips began to take on a life of their own. I rocked gently, back and forth, seeking more contact from his hand. Parting my legs wider, I gave him better access, a blatant invitation to explore anywhere he wanted.

Encouraged, Ransom's fingers slipped lower until he was touching my most intimate spot, making me writhe and moan.

"Ransom," I said breathlessly.

His lips went back to my neck, this time kissing me with more urgency as he began strumming me like a guitar.

I moaned, wanting him inside as his hands continued to pleasure me under the moonlight. In the reflection of the window, my body was a pale image against midnight black; I felt beautiful in a way I'd never thought possible.

Sexy, voluptuous, and wanton. And, truth be told, I liked what I saw. It turned me on even more.

Ransom pulled me back against him and away from the window. The bed was a few short steps to the right, and he steered us toward it. We collapsed into a tangle of arms and legs and then he pinned me to the mattress. His damp hair was a mess and his eyes were alive with hunger, making him look more like a wild, untamed animal. His mouth came down hard, parting my lips before exploring mine hungrily.

Fervently returning his kisses, I ran my hands through his hair, twisting it between my fingers. He growled against my mouth and palmed my breasts through the T-shirt. The growl deepened and was followed by the sound of ripping fabric.

Excited, I writhed beneath him, never having felt such desire for anyone.

Ransom's mouth found my breasts. My nipples tingled as he flicked his tongue around one and then moved to the other, sucking and teasing me into a frenzy. My body was on fire, arching against him… against this man… this beautiful… stranger.

A stranger.

I was suddenly hit with so much anxiety that all of my desire turned into fear and uncertainty.

I stiffened up. "Ransom…"

"Hmm?" he murmured, his lips still exploring my soft curves.

"Ransom…stop." I pushed against him.

He looked down at me with his heavy-lidded eyes and looked so sexy, I almost took it back.

"Stop?"

I nodded and met his gaze, expecting…I wasn't sure what to expect. Disappointment? Probably. Anger? Hopefully not.

He rolled onto his side, propping up his head with one hand, the other resting on my stomach. Fortunately, he didn't look angry. Just, disappointed. "What's wrong?"

I turned and stared off into the darkness. "I… just can't."

"Am I too sexy?" he joked. "Is it making you nervous?"

I laughed. He was sexier than hell and his sense of humor only added to it. "Yeah. Very."

Ransom's face grew serious. He made a slow circle across my stomach with his fingers. "Is it just too soon?"

"Yeah." I closed my eyes. I'd never cried over any of this, but tears threatened to fall now. I felt like I was out of control and it scared me more than Jordan himself. Being tracked. Chased. All of it. And now here was Ransom… opening up a whole new can of emotions. Jumping into bed with someone so quickly, even a guy who'd saved my life, was reckless. Maybe even dangerous, especially if I became pregnant. I didn't even know if he had any kind of protection with him.

"I don't know you well enough… yet… for this." I waved my hand over the bed. "I led you on. I'm sorry."

He reached up, caught my hand with his, and squeezed hard. "You didn't lead me on. And… I'm not Jordan, Hailey." Still holding my hand, he went on. "It's a trust issue. I'm a stranger, you don't even know my middle name. You don't want to get hurt. It makes perfect sense."

I stared at him with relief.

Ransom's eyes searched mine. "You're scared. Jordan's an ass. A *mean* ass motherfucker. I understand why you're frightened, especially about jumping into anything with a stranger."

"I thought it's what I wanted. And, I do. Just… not right now," I said. "I hope you're not too disappointed."

"I'd be lying if I said I wasn't because…well…" His eyes did a slow tour over my body. Everything he wanted—and he clearly wanted me—was reflected in his gaze. "I mean, who wouldn't want you?"

Feeling suddenly shy, I looked way.

Ransom tipped my chin up, so we were staring at each other again. "Hailey." The smile that played over his lips was all kinds of charming and disarming. "You're everything a guy could want in a woman. Not just sexually."

"You barely know me. How can you be so sure?" I whispered.

"There are some things a person just knows."

I smiled.

"Let's get some sleep." His eyes twinkled. "Just one more kiss, though. Then you're going to have to keep your hands to yourself *if…* you know what's good for you. I might be naked, but that doesn't make me easy."

I chuckled. "Okay, one more kiss and I'll try to control myself."

His lips on mine were soft and gentle, unlike the hard, demanding ones from earlier. He was so tender, that it took me completely off guard, even bringing tears to my eyes. I silently cursed my over-emotional state of mind.

"Hey." Ransom pulled back, looking down at me, confusion and concern flashing in his eyes. "What's wrong? I don't have to kiss you, if it's making you cry."

"It's okay. That's not why," I said, wiping away a couple of tears that had escaped. "It's just…" I gave him a frustrated smile. "I don't even know why I'm being a baby. This isn't like me at all."

I'd learned to keep a stiff upper lip and not feel sorry for myself. But, right then and there it felt like everything I'd managed to keep bottled up, was threatening to break free.

Ransom turned on the lamp. "You're not being a baby. Come, here."

He gathered me in his arms and held me against his chest, rocking me slowly. His gentle kindness brought a fresh wave of tears and this time, I gave in to them. Closing my eyes I sobbed, letting Ransom's body absorb all of the fear and pain that had been locked deep inside of me. Finally, I pushed him away, sniffling my way through the last of the tears.

"You okay?" he asked, staring at me with concern.

"Yes." I was embarrassed and wondered what he really thought of me now. "Thanks. I guess I needed that."

He smiled gently. "It was my pleasure. So, how about we get some sleep then?"

I struggled to sit up. "Sure. I'll just…" I swung my legs over the edge of the mattress, thinking I'd head somewhere other than the bed. But, guessing my intention, Ransom's arm went around my waist, holding me there.

"There's only one bed. We sleep here. Don't worry, I can control myself. Just make sure you do, too," he joked.

Smiling, I lay back down.

Ransom turned away, flicked off the lamp, then rolled back, pulling me against his chest. He was warm, solid, and still obviously aroused. I gingerly tried to pull away, to put a little space between the two of us. So, he could cool off. He wasn't having any of that, either, apparently.

"Where are you going?" he asked, his voice a low growl as he tightened his arms around my waist.

"Isn't this uncomfortable for you?"

"I'd rather spend an uncomfortable night and let you learn to trust me, than give up the chance to spend the night with you."

"Oh…" There was a beat of silence.

"You know, sex isn't everything," he murmured.

I burst into laughter. "That's not something I'd expect to hear from a guy. But, I'm glad you said it."

He rubbed my arm, the gesture at first comforting, but as his movements slowed, the touching turned to a caress. I felt the underlying sexual tension between us rising up again on both sides of the bed.

"Ransom…"

The hand stopped. "Yeah, I know. Sorry for pushing the envelope. I'll behave now. You can relax."

I settled my head on his shoulder. I had to admit, he made me feel safe, even if he was a pain in the ass. His promise to give me time with whatever this was between us, did far more to set me at ease than the head-butt he'd given Jordan. Or even the mad dash on the motorcycle.

Ransom's breathing eventually slowed and deepened. I listened to the sounds of him falling asleep and found it comforting. After a long time, I finally let myself relax, and drifted off.

8

Ransom

I woke up to the chirp of my cell phone. I knew it might be Reece and that he was probably worried sick, after yesterday. Not to mention, I hadn't shown up to work today. But, I wasn't ready to talk.

After a few more seconds, the ringing stopped and I rolled onto my side.

With my eyes still closed, I reached across the bed, encountering soft, warm flesh. Her hip. I wanted to slide my hand down that long, lovely thigh, or move upward, dip into the hollow of her waist, brushing against the heavy weight of her breast. But, I'd made a promise to her, and come hell or high-water, I'd keep it. So, I kept my hand where it was.

Given the unusual circumstances of the night before, I'd fallen asleep almost instantly, waking only half a dozen times or so. Hailey had been there each time, some part of her anatomy, warm and soft, pressed against my groin. Gritting my teeth a few instances, I'd managed to fall back asleep. Toughing it out now, until she grew to trust me, was the only thing I could do. I certainly wasn't going to take advantage of her. She'd been hurt too many times in the past and all I wanted to do was protect her. No matter what shade of blue my balls turned.

The phone started up again, and Hailey stirred beneath my hand.

"Yours or mine?" Her voice was sharp, with no sign of morning grogginess.

"Mine. Probably my boss." I sighed. "I suppose I should answer it."

"Good idea."

I grabbed my phone from the nightstand and answered it. "Yeah."

"Ransom? Where the hell are you? And what the hell have you done now?" barked Reece.

I groaned inwardly. He was obviously livid and I'd expected no less. "I'm… out of town. Vacation day."

Reece grunted and muttered a few colorful words.

I glanced over at Hailey, who was sitting up beside me now. Her knees were pulled up to her chest with the sheet wrapped tightly around her body.

"Bullshit answer. I repeat, what in the hell have you done?"

The fact that he was pretty much accusing me of doing something wrong irritated me. "I haven't *done* anything."

"Some asshole with a broken nose was here yesterday, looking for you. He said you took something that belongs to him."

I frowned and beside me, Hailey tensed. I glanced at her, my frown deepening. She could hear Reece and it was obviously scaring the hell out of her again.

"Really? Did he tell you what I supposedly took?"

"Damn it, Ransom, stop playing games!" Reece's voice dropped. "He was a shifter. You know exactly what the hell I'm talking about."

"Yeah. Well, it's complicated, okay? How did he find the shop, anyway?"

"He said someone at the diner recognized you, remembered the bike, then he tracked you back here."

I sighed. "Great. What else did he say?"

"He said you were a dead man." Reece laughed coldly.

"And why is that funny?" I asked dryly.

"It's just that he was such a cocky little bastard and all covered in blood. Not to mention, wearing that damn sissy suit. Couldn't really take him seriously right then. I actually kicked his ass out of the shop." The laughter trailed off. "Of course, now it appears that you're going to be in deep shit with Malone."

Our Alpha.

My stomach dropped. "He knows?"

"I believe so. If he hasn't, when he finds out you've pissed off another clan's Alpha, or at least that Alpha's son, he's not going to like it. You know nothing good can come out of this. I'm gonna ask you again, Ransom, what did you do?"

I turned to Hailey, who looked worried. "I helped someone who needed me, Reece. And... I'd do it again in a heartbeat."

"Yeah, but—"

"I gotta go. I'll call you later." I then hung up on him. He obviously didn't understand and I was tired of being lectured. I turned off the ringer, knowing I'd be getting more phone calls.

"Jordan found you...that means he'll find me." Fear coated Hailey's voice.

I tossed the phone onto the floor and turned back to her. "No. Reece doesn't know where I am. He doesn't even know about the cabin."

"He's not just your boss, though, right? He's part of your clan."

"Yeah. He's family. But not part of my *real* family." I shrugged. "You're not the only one with a complicated life. Most of my original clan is dead. Reece took me in when I was a teenager. We're not related by blood, but he's like a father to me."

"So, you're adopted?"

"Sort of. This cabin was owned by my real family and passed down to me. It's my safe haven. Anyway, I've been coming here since I was a kid. Reece doesn't know about it," I repeated.

"Is there a reason why you didn't tell him about it? Don't you trust him?"

"I trust Reece with my life, and have done so many times. Probably will again. But this…" I looked past her at the small cabin strewn with clothes, and the remnants of last night's dinner, taking it all in. "You know how when you have something you love, something you've shared with one other person? And then that person is gone, and all you have left is that special thing? *This* is the last thing I shared with my dad."

"And if you shared it with Reece, then it wouldn't belong to just you, and your dad?"

I smiled. "Yeah. Something like that."

Hailey reached out and took my hand. "But now you've shared it with me." Her voice was soft.

I nodded.

"And that changes things? I mean, with the cabin?"

"It does. But in a different way."

"How?"

I stared at her. Hailey's eyes were different in the morning light, the black edge softer, the lashes a dark sable against her pale skin. The tantalizing thought passed through my mind: how many other things were there to discover about Hailey?

"Ransom… different how?" she asked.

It took a considerable force of will to pull my mind back from the depths of her eyes. "I wanted to share this with you. I'm not sure why, but I just did. I know we barely know each other, but there is something about you that makes me want to trust you in a way that I haven't ever trusted another shifter. Or anyone, for that matter."

Her eyes filled with tears.

I pulled her against me. "That was supposed to make you feel better, not make you cry."

She laughed and wiped some of the moisture from under her eye. "I haven't exactly met a man like you before. Or trusted anyone, either. Not since I was a little girl."

She certainly wasn't a child anymore.

My eyes slipped slowly down from her face, lingering somewhere else. The sheet had slipped from her shoulders, one breast partly uncovered, round and full. If that wasn't sexy enough, her hard nipple poked against the sheet and my groin flexed in response.

"Anyone ever tell you how beautiful you look in the morning?" I murmured.

She smiled.

My eyes dropped to Hailey's mouth, taking in the contours of her full lips. Her lower lip was plump, just a bit fuller than the top. I suddenly had the urge to run my tongue across that lip.

I leaned forward and kissed her softly.

Hailey let out a sigh, but didn't pull back. Instead, she kissed me back, with fire and passion.

I lost myself completely as our mouths explored each other's. After a long, long time I pulled away, looking down at her. I knew what I wanted, but didn't want to rush her. Especially after last night. She needed time and I would give her whatever she needed.

"We should probably stop before…"

Her eyes sparkled. "We don't have to stop."

"Are you sure?"

"I… don't want to," she said, her cheeks turning pink.

More than anything, I wanted Hailey. Hearing her words sent a torrent of emotions through me.

9

Hailey

The fire Ransom had lit, fed, and fanned roared up inside me. I reached up and wound my fingers into his hair before pulling his lips back down to mine. Everything felt right, his body on mine. His hand moved over my skin, making me pant with desire. His mouth worked its magic as he moved lower, kissing my breasts and teasing my nipples. Moaning, I ran my hands running over his back, sliding down to his waist before cupping his taut ass. I was on fire and ached to have him inside of me. I was about to tell him when someone's cell phone beeped, startling us both.

Ransom broke away from me with a rough gasp.

"Yours or mine?" I asked after finding my voice.

Ransom nodded toward my stuff. "This time it's not me. Your duffel bag is ringing."

Tension flooded through me, a rush of adrenaline replacing arousal.

Who was calling now?

I scrambled off the bed, retrieved my phone, and sat on the floor. I looked at the screen and recognized the phone number. I swallowed and looked at Ransom. "It's him. Jordan. He must have gotten my new number."

Ransom sat up, the sheet pooling around his waist. "Don't answer it."

I thought about Keri and Glen. They were the only two people who had my number. If Jordan also had it now, he wouldn't have asked for it nicely. "I think I'd better," I said, dreading the conversation. "Hello?"

"Hailey. I know where you are." Jordan's voice was like a knife through my heart.

"How would you... you don't know where I am. You're bluffing."

"Do you want to take that chance? You and that brute who helped you are holed up. It's just a matter of time..."

I began to tremble. What if he really did know where we were? He was an excellent tracker. "Leave me alone."

"You're mine. I'm never leaving you alone," he growled.

"Hailey, hang up," Ransom said in a stern voice.

I glanced over at him.

He grabbed the phone from me and did it himself. "We need to leave."

"But why? He's lying. He couldn't possibly know where we are, right?"

Ransom pulled on a pair of jeans. "Get dressed."

I stood up, clutching my shirt. "What if he's just trying to scare me? This place is obviously off of the grid. You said so yourself. Nobody knows about it."

He scowled. "It's much more than that. Did he have your phone number before? No. He found it... got it from somewhere. Probably beat the hell out of someone at the diner."

"So? They couldn't have told him about this place."

Not saying anything, Ransom yanked a T-shirt over his head and then sat on the edge of the bed.

"We shouldn't jump just because of a phone call, Ransom," I said, as he pulled on his boots.

He glanced up, brows drawn together. "You said Jordan's father has friends in high places. I'm assuming even though they've got connections, back in the Old Country, they're a little more up-to-date with technology."

I frowned.

Ransom stood and looked down at me. His face softened and he reached out to put his hands on my shoulders. "Think about it. They probably ran some kind of a trace when he called you. Jordan really may know where we are right now."

My heart skipped a beat. I hadn't thought of that. "Oh… great."

"Get dressed. We're going to need to leave here. He'll be tracking us soon."

I nodded and quickly picked up my things.

Ransom grabbed his backpack and I watched him stuff clean clothes into it while I dressed.

From the floor, Ransom's phone began to vibrate. He walked over and picked it up.

"Reece," mumbled Ransom. "I suppose I'd better answer it after that last call from Jordan."

I nodded.

10

Ransom

"Yeah?"

"Ransom, you're in a world of hurt, and I'd appreciate it if you didn't hang up on me this time," said Reece.

I sighed. "I really don't have time…"

"Yeah, you *do* have time to listen to me. Things have been happening here. Calls… back and forth. Even worse, Malone just left here."

"And?"

"And he's got a message for you: back off. Leave her where she is, and come home. This isn't your fight."

I turned to the big window, watching the pines swaying in the breeze. Something in Reece's voice made the hair on the back of my neck stand up. The last thing I needed was someone telling me what to do. Even if that someone was Reece.

"Why the hell does Malone care about what I do?"

"Has she told you who she is? Who her Alpha is?"

"What the hell do I care who he is?"

"Well, Malone cares. Her Alpha heads one of the oldest clans on the East Coast and is someone who is still highly connected back in the Old Country. Apparently, this guy doesn't take kindly to strangers interfering with family business. He doesn't want to cause tension between us and them. You have to back off. Or…"

"Or what?"

Reece became quiet and the silence went on far too long for my liking.

"Or what, Reece? What are you trying to say?"

"There are things that happened before you came here. Things no one wants to dredge up."

"And what does that have to do with Hailey?"

Her head jerked up at the sound of her name.

I turned my back to her, even though I knew damn well she could still hear the conversation.

"More than you know. Ransom, Travis is the guy who had your whole clan killed."

Shock, followed by hot, boing rage filled me. "And he had my father killed too, I suppose?" I growled, when I found my voice.

Reece took a deep breath. "Yeah, I'm afraid so. But it's much more complicated than that. He didn't kill your father. He killed the man who you *thought* was him… the man he wanted out of the way." There was another pause.

All of the blood rushed to my head. *What in the hell was he saying?* "What is that supposed to mean?"

"The man you thought was your dad? He wasn't your real father. Ransom. I hate telling you this over the phone; it was something I wanted to tell you face-to-face once I found out about it. I'm so sorry, but Travis, Jordan's father… is also yours."

11

Hailey

After hanging up with Reece, Ransom sat silently on the edge of the bed, just staring out the window. I'd heard the conversation and could barely believe it myself.

I knelt beside him, aching to do something, *anything*, to help him. But my mind was just as jumbled, as I supposed, his was. If someone had told me that my father wasn't who I thought he was, I'd be a basket case. And to learn that the man we were running away from was your brother, or half-brother... well, it was all too much.

"Ransom?" I laid my hand on his shoulder. He didn't move. "Ransom, we need to go."

In response, he threw his phone across the room, making me flinch. It bounced against the bathroom door, skittering away across the tile.

"Did you hear?" he asked grimly.

I nodded.

He ran a hand through his hair. "What a mess. What a fucked up mess."

"Ransom, I'm sorry. Really... I don't know what else to say."

He turned and I saw so much pain and confusion in his eyes, it made my own heart ache.

"All these years, the man who raised me, I thought he was my father. Now I find out it's the guy who sired that prick, Jordan. My fucking brother." His laugh was sharp and cold. "How did this even happen? How did I meet you, only to find that my family is out on the hunt for you? How can this even be possible? It all seems too crazy… so contrived."

"I know; it's surreal. I can't believe it myself…"

"So, you didn't know?" Ransom turned to me suddenly, his eyes searching mind. Almost… accusingly. "Was that why…?"

"No," I said sharply before he even finished.

He frowned.

"How could I? I had no idea Jordan wasn't Travis's only son. No one ever talked about any other kids. I only just met you. How could I possibly know? You're not making any sense."

His eyes softened. "Yeah, I know… I'm sorry. It's just all too much." He shook his head absently. "I guess we'll just chalk this one up to fate, huh? Our paths crossing when they did?"

I sat back, wishing I had the magic words that would make this all go away. Or at least make it something we could understand. But, even if I believed in magic, I really didn't think there was enough to fix this situation.

"Yeah, fate… I'm in such shock about all of this, Ransom. And I'm so very sorry I got you involved."

He stood abruptly. "You didn't. I involved myself, and despite all of this bullshit, I don't regret it. I wanted to make sure you were safe, and that's still my focus. But you're right; we have to leave."

I got off the bed quickly and pulled on my shirt. Meanwhile, Ransom grabbed the backpack, scooped up his cracked phone, and shoved it into his pocket.

"Does it even work anymore?" I asked.

"I don't know or care right now," he muttered. "Let's just get out of here."

"Where are we going?"

"I'm not sure—" Ransom's words cut off abruptly. His head jerked up and his eyes locked on the door.

My heart skipped a beat. "What?" I whispered.

He went completely rigid and let the backpack fall to the floor. That's when I heard it. The sound of footsteps on the steps.

Panic gripped me and my heart leaped into my throat. I whirled, still fumbling with the buttons on my shirt.

The door abruptly splintered inward.

I gasped.

Jordan stood in the ruined doorway, his hands clenched into fists by his side. He was quite a sight with his nose, which appeared to be broken, and eyes that were black and blue. He gave us a maniacal grin. "Honey, I'm home!"

I took a step backward. "How… how are you here so quickly?"

He ignored my question. "Let's go." His voice was cold, but his eyes were animated, almost dancing with an evil inner light.

"No," I said firmly. As frightened as I was, I had faith in Ransom's abilities to protect me. Even now he stood poised to attack Jordan.

"Hailey, I'm not leaving without you. Get your ass over here. Now," Jordan demanded.

Ransom moved in front of me. His shoulders were broad and he towered over Jordan. "If you know what's good for you, you'll turn around and walk away."

Jordan glared at him. "Do you have any idea of who you're dealing with?"

"Yeah, an asshole who doesn't know when to quit."

He gritted his teeth. You've crossed the line, asshole and… you're going to pay. Now, get out of my way. I'm here for what's mine. She is mine, you know. Not yours. As a Lycan, you should know what happens when you take someone's mate."

Ransom glared at him. "She doesn't belong to anyone, especially *you*. Now, get the fuck off of my property."

Jordan erupted with a growl, lunging across the room toward Ransom.

I stumbled backward as Ransom shielded me with his body and easily sidestepped Jordan's clumsy rush.

Missing his target, Jordan crashed into the kitchen table. Furious, he spun around, knocking over the empty wine bottle from the night before. It hit the floor with a crash, leaving a welter of shattered glass.

"You're dead," he growled.

In that instant, Ransom began to morph into his Lycan form. I'd seen others shift… hell, I did it myself. But with Ransom, it was a force of nature. Strangely beautiful. Mesmerizing. Savage. His transformation was more like a magician's illusion. Now, where a man once stood, was a huge, powerful, white and gray wolf-beast. One that would have given his birth-father a run for his money.

I glanced over at Jordan, who was crouched by the counter. He was breathing hard and his lips were pulled back over his teeth. He seemed just as shocked by the rapid transformation as I was. Of course, not nearly as impressed with it. Unsurprisingly, he looked enraged. Angrier than I'd ever seen him.

Ransom lunged at Jordan, his nails gouging the hardwood floor. He hit him low, just above the knees. The blow dropped Jordan to the floor and Ransom pinned him down.

I waited for Jordan to change. Expected him to. But he remained in his human form. He was obviously crazier than I thought if he believed he could win a fight against a massive wolf-beast. Ransom outweighed him. Would outmaneuver him. Could tear out his throat with one bite, if necessary.

Jordan's hands wrapped around Ransom's throat and his fingers buried into his fur. It was enough to keep Ransom's snapping fangs away from his own throat, however. That was when I saw it. The shard of glass in Jordan's hand.

I gasped. "Ransom! Look out! He's…"

Before I could even finish the words, Jordan viciously stabbed Ransom's side with the glass several times, drawing blood

Ransom yelped in pain.

"Ransom!" I screamed.

Jordan shoved him away and then got back to his feet. This time he charged after me, a determined look on his face.

Stunned and terrified, I backed up, hitting the edge of the bed with my legs. I wanted to shift, but knew Jordan could overpower me easily, as he had so many times before.

Jordan grabbed my arm and pulled me toward the door.

"No!" I hollered, wrestling to get away. But, his grip was like steel.

Annoyed and frustrated that I was fighting back, Jordan lifted me feet off the floor and carried me to the door.

"Ransom!" I dug my nails into Jordan's arm, straining to see over his shoulder.

Was he okay?

I saw Ransom spring to his feet. Baring his fangs, he growled loudly and prepared to pounce.

Jordan spun around, using me as a human shield. I felt Jordan's body begin to shift, his muscles rippling, growing tense and hot. The familiar black fur began to sprout out of his skin and his claws began to appear.

"Move, and she dies." Jordan's distorted voice, half-human, half-growl, filled the room. "It's that simple."

I shuddered, remembering the countless times he'd threatened to kill me, and almost had. Yes, Ransom was bigger and probably more powerful. But, he was hurt. Just how badly, I didn't know.

My eyes met Ransom's and his gleamed with rage as Jordan wrapped his paw around my throat. Claws dug into my skin painfully drawing blood.

"One little slip and she's dead," Jordan threatened.

Ransom was still crouched on the floor in front of me and our eyes met. In his I saw anger. Frustration. Doubt.

"That's right, asshole. Be a good animal, and stay where you are," Jordan growled.

Ransom didn't move.

Jordan backed up through the busted-out doorway and into the cool morning air.

Ransom advanced slowly after us, hackles raised and growling low. His eyes flickered between mine and Jordan's, eventually locking back onto mine as Jordan dragged me toward the stairs.

"You just keep your distance," warned Jordan. "You piece of shit."

Ransom growled even louder.

Grunting, Jordan threw me over his shoulder, turned and jumped down the stairs, and then sprinted away on two legs. With surprising speed, he bolted through the woods, crashing down the same path I'd traveled with Ransom the night before.

"Let me go!" I screamed, hitting him with my fists.

I knew he was close to shifting fully and barely holding on to his human form. He knew if he let me go, there was a chance that I'd escape. I might have been weaker, but I was faster and he knew it.

Suddenly, we broke through the trees and into a clearing. I didn't see Ransom's motorcycle, but instead saw a bright red Ferrari parked alongside of the road. Jordan had taken a different trail, not the same one Ransom had used. He flung me against the car, pinning me with one hand, as he yanked open the driver's side door.

"Get your ass in the car. And don't bother shifting. We both know you're a slow shifter. Not to mention a worthless fighter. I could kill you in a heartbeat."

If you could catch me.

But, he was right. It took me too long to shift and I'd be vulnerable in the process.

Jordan pushed me hard.

I clambered over the gear shift, banging my elbows and knees, ending up crouched in the passenger seat. I couldn't resist reaching for the door handle, however.

Seeing the movement, Jordan grabbed my arm and twisted it painfully, his claws digging into my skin.

I cried out in pain and tried to get out of his vice-like grip.

"Don't even think about it." He leaned close, his breath hot and fetid.

I turned away.

Jordan grabbed my face with his other hand and forced me to look at him. The pads of his fingers, now more like paws, were rough against my skin. Sharp claws grazed my cheek. "You think you're getting away? Guess again."

"Why not just kill me and get it over with? We both know that's what you really want," I spat through clenched teeth.

Jordan's eyes darkened. He pulled me even closer and I cringed, desperate to get away from him. His breath was foul, as if he'd been eating something rotten, or was rotting from the inside out. Something was wrong. Really wrong. This scenario seemed more than just being in a car with a guy I'd jilted. One who happened to be poised between human and shifter.

"You're right. But, my father… you remember him? Your Alpha? The one you show no respect for? He wants you back. It's not what I want…"

His bloodshot eyes bored into mine, then his gaze slid down my face to my torn shirt. Something passed through his crazed eyes. Or… left them.

My heart skipped and it took me only a second to realize that the last shred of sanity Jordan had been clinging to had just deserted him.

His mouth curled into a bizarre smile, fangs competing with teeth, a grin that would have frozen Hell. "You know what? Fuck my father." His voice dropped lower and became an almost seductive purr, his eyes raking hungrily over my body. "Fuck you, too, while we're at it."

My breath froze in my throat and I struggled against the iron grip of his hand. But he was too strong, and for a horrible moment, I saw my immediate future. It wasn't pretty.

12

Ransom

Even back in my human form, I had been able to still smell the little prick's scent. It had burned my nose, coated the back of my throat, and made me want to cough.

Wincing, I rubbed my ribs where Jordan had stabbed me with the glass. Fortunately, I'd been smart enough to keep a first-aid kit at the cabin and had bandaged myself up quickly. Lycan healed fairly quickly, but he'd gotten me good and I was still in a world of pain.

By the time I reached the clearing, and my bike, I'd picked up on the scent of both Jordan and Hailey. It blew from the south.

I climbed onto the motorcycle and started it. Knowing they were getting away, I dropped it into gear. The rear tire spit up gravel as I tore up the road and toward the other route, where their scent was coming from. In no time, I hit the pavement, twisted the throttle, and took off at top speed down the mountain.

I knew the road like the back of my hand, and the bike screamed around the first corner. I'd learned to ride on the snaky roads, and was confident I could catch Jordan, no matter what kind of high-powered car he was driving.

13

Hailey

Jordan buried his head against my neck, his mouth hot against my skin. His teeth raked across my flesh and I cried out as I fought to push him away. But the car was too small, and he was too strong.

"Please, stop," I choked, trying to shove his hands away.

Suddenly, his head rose and he pushed me away roughly. "Hear that? That asshole has your scent." He snorted an ugly sound. It was then that I heard the unmistakable sound of a motorcycle roaring to life.

I allowed myself to take a breath.

Jordan glared at me and tilted his head. "I bet you got him to give you a ride, bring you here, all by giving that animal just what he wanted. Just with a swing of those hips of yours. What *I* wanted. What was mine. What you never gave me."

His words made my sick. "You're fucking crazy, Jordan. Ransom isn't…"

My head snapped back as his hand connected with my cheek. My cheekbone felt like it was on fire, but I gritted my teeth and turned toward the window. Jordan pounced on any sign of weakness. It fed whatever drove him to hurt. Crying could send him into a frenzy. It wasn't something I wanted to experience in such a confined space.

"Do *not* call me crazy…" He turned the key in the ignition, cutting off the rest of his words.

I closed my eyes, swallowed hard, and leaned my forehead against the cold glass of the window. Jordan's nasty remark stung.

Had I played on the chemistry between us and used it to my advantage? And then shut Ransom down?

Right now, I wasn't even sure of the answers.

My eyes flew open as the car rocketed onto the narrow road. Jordan loved his cars, and the Ferrari was one of his favorites. Now, on the narrow, twisting mountain road, he took the curves at top speed, the car slewing from lane to lane.

"Like the view?" He flung the car around a corner, and I looked out the window, over what seemed to be a thousand-foot drop, straight down. The guardrail flashed past, the car barely missing the metal that was supposed to keep us from hurtling to certain death. Jordan's high-pitched laughter filled the car, as I white-knuckled the door handle.

"You're going to get us both killed."

"Shit," he growled, ignoring me. "Fucking bastard."

I tore my eyes away from the view to find Jordan glaring at the rearview mirror. Without turning, I knew who was behind us. I looked into the side mirror and my heart, which was already hammering, skipped a succession of beats.

Yes. It was Ransom.

Part of me had thought he might give up and go back to his clan. But, Ransom had followed us. He'd come for me, after all.

14

Ransom

The bike screamed beneath me, giving sound to my fury. I hunched lower, taking another series of turns at high speed, and caught the flash of a red car ahead, hugging the guardrail. The sun glinted off the passenger side window before the car dipped into a patch of shade. For a brief moment, I saw the outline of Hailey's head.

She was alive.

At least sitting upright in the passenger seat. I'd feared that Jordan had decided to kill her and it was a relief to see that she wasn't dead.

But other fears also rose in my mind. Once Jordan saw me following, would he unleash his rage on Hailey? Or… would his already reckless driving escalate until he lost control? What if the car crashed into the mountain or plummeted over the edge and into the valley below?

I let up on the throttle, dropping back. There was nowhere for him to go, other than down the mountain. If he took any of the side roads, he'd be forced to drop his speed. That didn't seem like something Jordan would do. I had to be patient, not lose sight of the car, but not push him too hard.

As I dropped back even more, my mind raced over every possibility. That was when Reece's warning came back to me. Along with the admission that Travis was the person who'd sired me. A ruthless and dangerous killer in his own right.

My father… the man who would always be that to me, regardless of blood… had been murdered at the base of this mountain. It had been staged to look like a trail accident. Except… my father didn't really hike. Sure, he enjoyed the wilderness, but most of the exploring took place at night and in his Lycan form. Not during the day. I'd known it was murder right from the get-go. Reece, too. But, no one in the clan, besides myself, had seemed interested enough to find out what happened. And when I had tried asking questions, they'd been brushed off. So, in the end, it all just got covered up. Buried. Never talked about again.

Could Jordan be taking Hailey to the same spot?

Did he know Travis had killed a man there?

The Ferrari roared out of sight around the next corner. I knew there was a cut-off road not far ahead. It was really nothing more than a muddy dirt track that came out below where my father was killed. If I could make it through, and if the road wasn't washed out…with any luck, I'd be able to get there before them. I could hide the motorcycle, and wait.

But, what if I was wrong?

I could lose her. Maybe even forever.

Gritting my teeth, I decided to go for it. Something inside urged me toward that decision. I'd learned that my gut was pretty reliable, and it was all I had at the moment.

The road was rutted, and I was forced to slow the bike down, veering around potholes and a fallen tree. Finally, it became a mire of mud, completely impassable.

I got off and pushed my motorcycle into the thick cover of rhododendron that grew along the sides. As I put down the kickstand, I could hear the roar of a sports car in the distance, and relief flooded through me.

Thank God. My hunch had been right.

With my heart hammering in my chest, I sprinted down the road, the highway visible through the screen of overhanging trees. I was about twenty feet from the end of the road when the red car flew past.

Fuck!

I slid to a halt in the slick mud. I'd been too slow. Jordan was going to get to the trail ahead of me. I wasn't going to be able to save Hailey after all. I'd failed her… again.

15

Hailey

I watched in the side mirror, as we hurtled down the road, and caught an occasional glimpse of Ransom crouched low over the Harley. Each time I saw him, he was a little closer, and it was hard controlling the excitement that bubbled up inside.

But then, suddenly, he dropped back.

I straightened, frowning as the car shot forward and Ransom disappeared. Swiveling in the seat, I looked back over my shoulder as we rounded yet another curve. In the distance, I saw him again and watched in disbelief as he slowed, turned the bike off the road, and disappeared into the underbrush.

"Looks like lover-boy gave up on you, Hailey. Finally came to his senses." Jordan's nasty laugh filled the car. He reached across the console, grabbing my knee. "You're back with me, baby. Just where you belong."

"I'm not yours." I dug my nails into Jordan's hand, wanting to hurt him like his words hurt me.

Unfazed, he laughed again, giving my knee a cruel pinch.

I slumped back into the seat, moving as far away from Jordan as I could in the cramped space. I felt hopeless and wondered if this really was the final straw for Ransom. If being bested by Jordan would make him throw up his hands and turn back toward his old life. I couldn't exactly blame him. This whole "save-the-damsel-in-distress" gig was probably turning out to be so much more than what he had bargained for.

Along with that, his involvement with me had uncovered his true father. Not to mention the terrible fact that Jordan was his half-brother. No matter how much chemistry we'd had, I didn't think it was enough to overcome everything that had happened to Ransom in the past twenty-some hours. Fate, or bad luck. I was betting he would probably pick the second option.

As my thoughts raced, Jordan kept the car at top speed, still swinging from lane to lane. The terrain had changed, the road leveling out, although the twists and turns continued.

Suddenly, he braked and I jerked forward, slamming my hands against the dashboard. The car skidded violently, almost sliding into the shallow ditch. The stench of burning rubber and brake pads filled the vehicle.

"What the hell? Are you trying to kill *both* of us?" I turned to Jordan but he ignored me and scanned the roadside.

"This must be it," he muttered and turned off the engine. Jordan looked at me. "Get out. And don't run. You know damn well I can catch you. Not that I wouldn't enjoy the chase, but I don't have time to waste."

Right, I thought. Running might be my only option.

I opened the door and stepped out into the briars that filled the ditch. Waiting for me to pick my way through them appeared to be too much for Jordan. He came around the front of the car, grabbed my arm, and pulled me by force up to the pavement.

"Move your ass, Hailey." He pushed me ahead of him, and I stumbled onto the chipped edge of the pavement.

"Asshole," I muttered, waiting for the right moment to shift and run like hell. If I had any chance at escaping, I needed to do it when he wasn't paying attention.

"Do I have to carry you? I will, you know." He grabbed my elbow and forced me down the road.

I tried in vain to grab the front of my shirt, to pull the tattered edges together over my bra, but Jordan had my arm wrenched almost to shoulder height. Finally, I gave up, letting my shirt flap in the breeze.

"Where the hell are you taking me?" I asked.

"It's a surprise." Jordan's voice was harsh. Cruel. His breath rasped from his throat and it was clear he was again desperately trying to hold on to his human form. He'd been more or less human on the ride down the side of the mountain. Whatever the hell was wrong with him, it was bad. *Scary* bad. Like nothing I'd ever seen before.

Suddenly he pushed me down the side of the road, toward a scarlet trail-marker nailed to a tree. I lifted my head, looking up the steep trail, then beyond at the bulk of the mountain rising above us. We were at the bottom of the mountain, the *same* mountain where Ransom's cabin was. I was pretty certain it was the trail he'd mentioned that ran below it.

But why in the hell would Jordan drag me back to where he'd taken me from?

Jordan pushed me hard from behind, and I stumbled down the narrow dirt path.

"Jordan, where are we going? What are you doing?" I asked, glaring back at him.

"We're going to wherever I take you. And as far as what I'm going to do? Well, you'll just have to wait and see."

I tried talking him into letting me ago and it only aggravated him more.

"Shut up and move," he growled, pushing me forward with so much force that I tripped and fell onto a collection of rocks. One of them was so sharp and jagged that it cut into my leg, causing me to bleed.

"Clumsy bitch." Jordan grabbed my arm, jerking me back to my feet. "Don't worry, though. Soon, I'm going to put you out of your misery."

Gritting my teeth, I limped several more yards down the trail, cold fear pooling in the pit of my stomach. Besides that, my heart hurt thinking about Ransom. Or, rather, trying not to think about him and how abandoned I felt.

"Here. Stop here." Jordan shoved me hard again.

This time I fell forward onto my hands and knees. I hung my head and clenched my teeth. "So, this is it? You're going to just kill me here in the woods?"

"This just isn't some random place, Hailey," he said with a smile in his voice. "It's a very special one. You see, someone else met their end here. Now… you will, too."

I looked up at Jordan. I was so tired. I didn't even have the energy to try and escape anymore. What was the use? Even if I got away, I would always be running from this sick asshole and his psycho father. It was exhausting. "Why? Why me? I left you at the altar…did I embarrass you so much that you actually want to kill me?"

"You're a little person in a big world, Hailey. I was willing to forgive you. Hell, to even take you back. But now… now you're involved in something much bigger. You… and that animal of yours. You need to disappear, and so does he. I'm… almost sorry." He leaned over, and to my surprise, caressed my cheek.

I flinched.

His face turned dark. Scowling at me, he cupped my chin roughly and tilted it up. "I'm going to kill you. Then… I'm going to kill him."

16

Ransom

After shifting into my Lycan form, I tore through the forest, my paws barely hitting the ground. The trail was just ahead, and I caught a whiff of Hailey's scent. She was hurt. Bleeding. I just couldn't tell how badly. The hot, coppery scent of her blood sent my rage at Jordan to an almost uncontrollable level. The bastard had hurt her and I was going to make sure he never had the chance to do it again. No to anyone.

As I moved closer, I could hear Jordan's voice. I slowed, making sure to stick to the thickest areas of underbrush and shrubs. The trail wasn't that far ahead, and I didn't want to lose the element of surprise. I was pretty certain Jordan saw me following them on the road. I could only hope he believed I'd given up the chase.

I crouched low, slinking forward as I moved closer. Glimpses of Jordan's white shirt, now streaked with blood and dirt, were visible through the bushes. I moved forward, peering through a screen of leaves, and that was when I saw Hailey. She was on her hands and knees, and blood seeped through the leg of her jeans. Jordan paced in front of her, his face contorted by his broken nose, and that sick, hideous grin he wore. I watched him closely. It was obvious the guy was on edge again, barely able to control his body. And, I suspected, his emotions.

That bothered me.

If the guy wanted to shift, why didn't he?

He hadn't shifted at the cabin, either. Something either kept Jordan from shifting, or kept him from completely holding on to his human form. A memory tugged at the back of my mind. A quick flash of firelight. Back when I was a small boy, listening to my father talk about something… similar. Before I could grasp anything else, it was gone.

I brushed it off. Now wasn't the time to figure out what was wrong with the guy, anyway. Jordan's voice had already risen, his tirade continuing. If I didn't do something, chances were pretty good he'd hurt Hailey again. Why else did he have her here?

I waited until Jordan's back was to me, then crept to the edge of the trail. I tensed… watching. Waiting. He was yelling at her now, his face very close to hers. Hailey was still on her knees, hunched over, looking up at him. From the look on her face, I could tell she was giving up. That bothered me. Especially considering how strong of a woman she was. To see her looking so utterly defeated made me sick.

As I slowly circled behind Jordan, Hailey glanced up and saw me. There was a moment of relief on her face before her eyes snapped back to Jordan. Unfortunately, her expression gave everything away.

I growled a curse and then did the only thing I could do. I tensed, back legs coiled like a spring. Digging in and pushing off, I launched myself at Jordan.

17

Hailey

Jordan's rants were growing more and more incoherent as he paced in front of me. Somewhere, in all his yelling he'd accused me of not only leaving him at the altar, but of being the one responsible for the downfall of his entire clan.

"What do you mean? Just because I'm not marrying you, the clan is falling apart?" I didn't understand, and none of it made sense.

"Everyone thinks I'm weak. Unworthy to be the next Alpha. Even my own father doesn't think I'm good enough. I can tell by the way he looks at me," he ranted.

I watched him warily as he paced back and forth, going on and on about Travis and the others. His dirty shirt was stained yellow under the arms and clung to his chest, and trickles of perspiration ran down his forehead. He impatiently swiped a forearm across his face, wiping the sweat from his eyes. "With my luck, he'll push me aside and make dickhead the next Alpha. Which is why I need to make sure he disappears."

Movement behind Jordan distracted me.

Ransom!

He was there on the path, coiled and ready.

A sound escaped me, barely audible. I tried to bite it back, but it was too late. Jordan caught it. His tirade cut off in midsentence and he stiffened up.

Ransom lunged, and for a moment, everything slowed down. His taut, muscular body seemed to be suspended in mid-air as he leaped toward Jordan. His attack was completely silent. The sheer power in it took my breath away.

Alarm flashed in Jordan's eyes. He made a half-turn, stepping aside quickly enough that Ransom missed his mark. He hit Jordan in the shoulder and was thrown off balance to the side, away from him.

I watched as he back twisted around and saw the pain in Ransom's eyes. Remembering that he'd been stabbed, I wondered how critical the wound was and if he could even handle going against Jordan. Then my thoughts raced beyond Ransom.

What exactly was wrong with Jordan?

He was cold and calculating. The asshole I remembered. But now he was also a raving mad, half-human with bad breath and foul body odor. Even in the car ride, he'd been sweating like a pig. Had he gone completely crazy, or was there something physically wrong with him?

Ransom scrambled to his feet, pain replaced with a fierce anger.

A rough, guttural noise from Jordan caught my attention, and I watched him, eyes widening.

"Oh, my God," I whispered.

Jordan was changing, finally. But something was wrong.

Very wrong.

I'd seen Jordan shift many times. He certainly wasn't handsome in human form, but when he shifted, he became an extremely powerful Lycan. Now, something else was happening. And it wasn't pretty.

His limbs elongated, arms and legs contorting at odd angles. In fact, I could hear his tendons snapping and cracking. It looked… and sounded… hideously painful. A horrible imitation of a shifter changing. As I watched, Jordan threw his head back, a shrill cry coming from his mouth. Even Ransom seemed momentarily distracted by the awful display happening on the forest floor.

Jordan let loose one final shriek, before his body resolved into its final form. Something horrifying. His legs were misshapen. His body distorted. His coat was coarse and matted. The same putrid stench rolled off of him in waves.

Ransom and I looked at each other for a brief second, both of us in shock.

Jordan gave himself a final shake, his oversized head swinging on a long, gangly neck.

"What in the living hell?" I whispered, taking a step back.

The two beasts glared at each other with hackles raised, one of them perfect, the other a hideous mutant. I scrambled away from the pair, frightened of what was about to happen. Especially with Ransom hurt and having to face such a frightening opponent. But neither looked in my direction. They were locked onto each other and circling. Both stiff-legged and mirroring the movements of the other.

It was Jordan who made the next move, seemingly unable to contain himself. A low, ugly growl ripped from his throat as he dove at Ransom. His speed was incredible, but his attack was clumsy, rushed, and way off balance. He hit Ransom at a sharp angle, his body sliding alongside his and deflected by the larger Lycan's mass.

Ransom turned and clamped down on the back of Jordan's neck with a terrible crunch. Yelping, Jordan threw his head back and snapped his jaws over Ransom's shoulder, missing their mark by a long shot.

Ransom bore down, driving Jordan's forelegs into the ground.

I rose to my knees. It was all over; it had to be. I knew the power in a Lycan's jaws could snap the neck of any living thing, human or other shifter. Jordan's neck was thin, weak-looking. And Ransom was an immensely powerful beast.

But… it wasn't over.

I watched in horror as Jordan twisted beneath Ransom, kicking out with his back legs, hitting him in the midsection. Ransom let go of him, doubling over with a grunt.

Jordan scuttled away and my heart sank. He'd retaliated with a sucker punch onto Ransom's injured ribs. Fortunately, Jordan was also hurt and the act seemed to take what was left out of him. I watched the blood well out of the wounds on his neck, darkening his fur as it dripped onto the ground. He shook his head and let out a low whine.

Meanwhile, Ransom was in pain, but not yet beaten. He straightened up and charged again, this time hitting Jordan in his flank. I watched as his jaws sank into Jordan's soft underbelly.

Jordan bellowed. His head flung back and he caught the edge of Ransom's ear in his mouth. I winced, as teeth ripped through flesh and blood poured down the side of Ransom's face. Despite the attack, he held on by twisting his head, driving forward with his back legs, and pushing Jordan across the path into the dirt and leaves. He kept going until finally, he slammed Jordan against the trunk of a tree. There was a sickening crack; Jordan yelped in pain while thrashing violently in Ransom's grip.

During a wild scramble of fur and legs, teeth and claws, I watched in fear as Jordan wrenched himself free from Ransom's jaws. His body writhed, and I realized he was shifting back to human form, his body wavering between the two. Blood ran from gashes in his side and neck. Where the patchy, matted fur gave way to human skin, I saw bruises that were deep and bloody. If that wasn't bad enough, one front leg was twisted at an awkward angle and I thought I saw the white ends of bone protruding through dirty fur. Nausea and revulsion washed through me, but I never took my eyes off Jordan.

Jordan turned toward me, one hand now clenched in a fist.

"You bitch," he growled.

Shaking, I took a step backward.

He advanced. His cruel jaws snapped at me as the upper part of his face slipped into human form. For one heart-stopping instant I met his eyes, full of rage—and insanity.

"All of this... your fault, Hailey."

My name, choked out in that horrible half-growl, half-human voice, chilled me to the bone.

I almost thought Jordan was going to attack, but instead, he turned and disappeared into the forest.

Releasing my breath, I watched and listened to the dwindling sounds as he moved away from us. It was followed by silence.

"Hailey?"

I turned.

Ransom was crouched on the path, the side of his head bloody. It also covered his arms and the side of his body. A deep purple bruise covered the lower side of his chest.

"Ransom!" I ran over and knelt beside him, tentatively extending my hand. At this point, I wasn't even sure where the blood ended and Ransom began. "Are you all right?"

"I'm good. It's worse than it looks. It'll heal." He looked up and his eyes searched my face. "But we need to get out of here. Get me some clothes. Make sure you're okay. How's your leg?"

"It's fine. Nothing at all compared to your injuries. What are we going to do about Jordan? He's still out there."

"I don't think the asshole is coming back, at least for a while. He's got even deeper wounds to lick than I do."

I knew he was right, otherwise he would have attacked me.

Ransom got to his feet and took my hand. He scanned the forest and pointed toward the ridgeline. "The cabin is just above us on the trail. I know he's aware of it now, but it's the closest place."

"Okay."

18

Hailey

When we arrived back at the cabin, Ransom went in first.

"All clear," he called out, while I kept watch outside.

I stepped through the ruined doorway and found him pulling on a new pair of jeans he'd grabbed from his backpack.

He gestured toward the door. "I need to fix that. There's some plywood underneath the cabin." He zipped up his jeans. "Wait here."

Before I could say anything, he was out the door.

I turned toward the big window. From here, the trail we'd just climbed was visible as a faint line across the meadow. I watched it anxiously, expecting Jordan to appear, half-changed and covered in matted fur and blood. His wounds were bad, very bad, but it gave me cold comfort.

I jumped at the noise behind me and turned to find Ransom wrestling a large sheet of plywood into the cabin. He propped it over the doorway, blocking out the sunlight streaming in, and began hammering huge nails through the wood into the cabin walls. After he was finished, Ransom stepped back to admire his handiwork.

"There. That should slow him down if he tries to return. At least for a little while," Ransom said.

"Let's hope."

"Don't worry. You're safe with me, purdy lady," he replied, twirling the hammer like a gunslinger and then pretending to slide it into an imaginary holster.

I laughed and some of my anxiety dissolved. It felt good. "We need to get you cleaned up, Ransom. You're still bleeding," I said, looking at his ear. It was covered in blood and still looking pretty mangled.

He dropped the hammer onto the kitchen table as I tried pulling him toward the bathroom. "Eh. It's nothing. It's already starting to heal. It's you I'm more worried about."

I looked down at my bloody jeans. "Actually, mine is looking better already, too. But yours… we should probably take a look at it."

"Fine. If you insist. I have a first aid kit."

I followed him down the hallway and into the bathroom. He perched himself on the edge of the sink.

"It's in there." He nodded toward a cabinet in the corner of the room. "Pretty much everything you'll need."

I opened the door, startled by the array of boxes stocking the shelves. I grinned. "Expecting Armageddon? Or a zombie attack?" I pulled a bottle of alcohol and a package of gauze off one of the shelves, tearing open the wrapper with my teeth.

"None of those. But, I was a pretty wild kid and always getting hurt." He watched as I poured alcohol onto the gauze. "Let's just say that I climbed a lot of trees…and fell out of them."

"A regular Tarzan, huh?" I started dabbing the gauze against his ear.

Ransom gritted his teeth and made a noise. "That's good."

I chuckled. "You just fought off Jordan. You can handle a little rubbing alcohol."

"I guess we know why males don't get pregnant. We'd never handle the pain as gracefully as you."

"You got that right." I leaned forward and inspected his ear and the side of his face. True to his shifter nature, the wound was already beginning to heal and the blood left behind already drying. "It's already healing. Looks clean…"

"Good," he murmured softly.

I was suddenly aware of the nearness of Ransom's body, the heat of his skin, and the fact that my blouse still hung open.

"I could get used to this. You taking care of me," he said with a sexy grin that started a wave of delicious heat in my stomach.

"It's the least I could do, considering you saved my life." I let my eyes drift from his face, over his broad chest, and down to his six-pack. He truly was a sexy beast, in both human and Lycan form.

"I almost thought I'd lost you there for a minute," Ransom said, his face serious now. "I went crazy thinking about it."

"And I went crazy thinking that I'd never see you again. When you turned off on your motorcycle, I almost thought you'd…" my voice trailed off.

"Given up?" His eyes held mine. "Hailey, I would never do that."

"I wouldn't blame you if you changed your mind, though. Especially now that he's going to come back for me." We both knew it was only a matter of time. More than likely, Jordan would wait for his wounds to heal and try to take us by surprise, or call in reinforcements.

"Let him. Next time, he won't be able to run away. I'll take him down for good."

I swallowed.

"I will never let anyone hurt you again," he added, cupping the side of my face.

I closed my eyes, enjoying the warmth of his hand. His words made my heart flutter. I hadn't had anyone care about my welfare in a very long time. Or touch me the way he did.

"You're a good man, Ransom. How in the world did I get lucky enough to meet you?" I replied softly.

He stroked my cheekbone with his finger. "I wouldn't call it luck," he said with a smile in his voice. "I mean, wait until you get to know me more…"

I opened my eyes. "Speaking of which, maybe we should do that right now." I looked over at the shower.

Noticing, Ransom raised his eyebrow. "What are you saying?"

"Exactly what you think I'm saying."

He held my gaze for a moment. "You sure?"

After everything that had happened, I wanted to be as close to Ransom as I could be. Although we barely knew each other, the last few hours had brought us so close together, that I knew fate had a hand in it. This time. This moment. It was meant to be. *We* were meant to be.

"I've never been more."

He smiled.

"Although, do you think it's safe? I mean, Jordan needs to heal but… you don't think he'll show up anytime soon?"

"No, and I'm not saying that just to get you between the sheets."

I smiled. "I know you're smarter than that and wouldn't jeopardize our safety for sex. Why do you think he's not coming back? Because of how injured he was?"

"For one, I heard him start the engine to his car as we were leaving."

I sighed.

"For two, I don't think he'll face me again until he's healed."

I didn't think so, either. Ransom had already gotten the best of him twice, and now Jordan could hardly move. "What if he tries and brings back-up?"

Ransom frowned. "Do you think he will?"

I thought about it and shook my head. "I think he's too afraid of Travis and what he might do. He's supposed to bring me back to the clan, alive, and I don't think he has permission to kill you."

"You mean try to?" Ransom said dryly.

I smiled. "Yeah."

He slid off of the sink, his body close to mine.

I drew a breath, and got hit with a wave of Ransom's scent, a mix of sweat, blood, and arousal. He lowered his head and began kissing me. It was gentle but insistent, hinting at where he wanted to take me. And, where he wanted me to take him.

I rose up on my toes, seeking more from Ransom, wanting the kiss to be deeper. But he kept me reaching and on my toes, teasing me. His mouth curved against mine and I knew he was smiling at my frustration. Making me work for it.

Reaching up, I threw my arms around his neck and pulled him down to my level until he was right where I wanted him. His smile widened for a moment and then our kiss deepened.

His arms went around me, pulling me against his bare chest. The warmth of his skin against mine was intoxicating. I slid against him, the friction of his body against my bra-covered breasts sent shivering tingles through me. My nipples grew hard and tight and the heat in my belly spread throughout my body. The wanton lust hit me hard and fast. Overcome with an aching need for more, I moaned against his lips.

Ransom pulled away and looked down at me hungrily. "Let's take this to the shower?"

My womanhood tingled with anticipation.

I nodded and watched as he began unbuttoning his jeans. He'd seen me naked, but we were stone-cold sober now and I was suddenly feeling shy.

"Would you mind if I went in first?" I asked.

19

Ransom

"No. Go ahead," I replied.

"You'd think I wouldn't be modest after everything," Hailey said, walking over to the shower. She turned on the water.

"You don't have to apologize about anything," I replied. "Or be modest. You have a beautiful body."

She looked at me over her shoulder and I saw that her cheeks were flushed. "Thank you. Um, could you turn around?"

I did what she asked, but could still see her in the mirror. She removed what was left of the shirt and then took off her jeans. Next, it was her panties, and when I saw her bend down to remove them, I grew even harder. Finally, it was her bra. As it dropped to the floor, I felt the beast in my blood begin to awaken. I wanted her badly and didn't know if I'd be able to control myself again.

She stepped into the shower and drew the curtain shut.

Licking my lips, I quickly got undressed. "Ready for me?" I asked, my cock already hard and aching.

"Yes."

I pulled back the curtain and her eyes flew down to my hips.

"Wow," she said, her blush deepening.

"What?"

"It looks much bigger in the daylight."

Being a guy, I couldn't help but be proud. I'd had compliments before, but hers meant more to me.

"You're doing it to me," I said, staring hungrily at her, wet luscious curves.

Hailey moved aside so I could get in next to her. I pulled the curtain back and then reached for her.

"Wait, what about your ear?" she asked, looking anxious again.

"Only one thing aches right now." I slid my hands around her waist and pulled our hips together.

She reached down and touched the head of my cock, making me groan.

"See," I growled as Hailey's hand wrapped around the shaft and she gripped it tightly.

She looked up at me and her lip twitched. "Oh, you poor, baby."

Overcome with lust, my lips crashed down on hers and we began kissing again. She opened her mouth to mine and I explored hers hungrily. I could smell her arousal and it made it difficult to resist bending her over and taking her like an animal. But, I didn't want our first time to be standing up and in the shower. I wanted her underneath me. I wanted her on top of me. I wanted to watch her face as I made love to her like she deserved.

Pulling myself away from her lips, I stepped back and picked up the bottle of shower gel. "Let's get clean and take this out there before I get too excited."

She nodded.

I turned back to her and poured the gel onto her breasts. She began rubbing it over them when I stopped her and began doing it myself. Feeling her slippery, wet globes in the palms of my hands made me harder yet.

"I have other parts of my body that need to be cleaned," she teased as I squeezed and fondled her breasts.

Smiling, I grabbed the gel and poured some into my palms. I then began soaping up the rest of her body, somehow staying in control as my hands moved to her ass and then finally, the junction between her legs. She moaned as I rubbed the soap over her sex and slid my fingers between her slit, which was wet from her own juices. Licking my lips, I got down on my knees.

"What are you doing?" she asked, her voice hitched as she stared down at me.

"Checking my work," I murmured.

She gave me strange look and I had the feeling she really didn't know what I was about to do.

20

Hailey

Before I could stop him, Ransom leaned forward and began pleasuring me. Gasping, I leaned back against the wall and closed my eyes as he swiped his tongue against my most intimate parts, working me into a frenzy.

I pulled at his hair as his tongue lashed my clit. I arched into him, whimpering in ecstasy as he made me feel things I'd never felt before. A few short seconds later, he brought me over the edge into an orgasm that had me crying and laughing at the same time. When I was finally able to catch my breath, we took it to the bedroom. Once I was on the mattress, we started kissing again.

"Hailey," he murmured. "I want you so much."

"I want you, too."

With a fiery look in his eyes, he moved himself against me, pressing against my folds. Slowly, he entered my core, both of us gasping from the searing heat. He pulled out and plunged deeper and then again and again.

"Ransom," I moaned, meeting him thrust for thrust as our bodies and mouths moved together. Delicious friction penetrated every nerve. Although I wasn't a virgin, this was so much better than what I'd experienced before. My body felt like it was taking on a life of its own, arching and twisting beneath him as he hit my G-spot. The tension began to build again, winding me into a tight frenzy. I wanted release. I wanted this to go on forever. I wanted… everything.

It was Ransom who took me—pushed me—over the edge, by driving into me with animal fierceness. Molten pleasure pooled and then erupted into cataclysmic waves. I screamed as the force of the orgasm shook me and then left me feeling like a helpless ragdoll.

Ransom paused to kiss me before moving hard and fast, like a jackhammer. I stared into his blue eyes, catching a glimpse of the beast lurking just beyond, as he moved his hips. Everything about him was so sexy. So beautifully masculine. So erotic. It made me shiver.

With one final thrust, he groaned in pleasure and pulled out quickly, spilling his hot seed onto my stomach. It was unexpected, but I was grateful that one of us had been thinking. The last thing we needed was for me to get pregnant. Especially with Jordan on our backs.

After cleaning up, he wrapped his arms around me and we held each other. We stayed like that, locked in a quiet embrace, and it felt like I was home. Smiling to myself, I let out a breathy sigh.

"This *is* nice, isn't it?" he murmured against my hair.

"Yes."

He was quiet for a couple of minutes and then chuckled.

"What's so funny?"

"If someone would have told me a week ago that I'd be here, in this bed, with a woman, I'd have told them they were on crack."

"I know, right? I can't believe I'm here either."

"Do you… how do you feel about what just happened?" he asked. "Are you having any regrets?"

I turned around and looked into his eyes. "Only that we didn't meet sooner."

He smiled, kissed me again, and then closed his eyes.

Content, I closed mine, too. I couldn't sleep, though. As wonderful as everything was, at that moment, I knew we were taking too many risks by staying there.

"Can't sleep, huh?" he murmured after a while.

"No."

"Thinking about Jordan?"

"Yeah, unfortunately."

He opened his eyes. "Did you ever sleep with him?"

"No. He wanted to be my first, but… I never let him touch me."

In fact, I'd only had sex with one guy, a man named Shawn, whom I'd met while on the run. After dating for a couple of months, we ended up going all the way. Unfortunately, a week after, I'd learned that Jordan was getting close and needed to leave. Although I hadn't loved Shawn, I'd developed feelings for him and had been afraid of him getting hurt. So, I never contacted him again.

"Something is wrong with Jordan."

I grunted. "Many somethings."

"I mean physically, he's not right."

"I was wondering about that myself. It's like he can't shift all the way. It's almost like he's stuck."

Ransom nodded.

"It just doesn't make any sense, though, does it? We're immune to diseases, aren't we?" I'd never heard of a Lycan getting sick or having medical problems. We were healthy, unless someone harmed us physically, and *that* didn't even last forever. We were basically… indestructible.

"The human kind. Maybe he's contracted something we don't know anything about."

"So, you think it could be a virus or something?"

"I don't know. Let's hope not."

And then it hit me and the blood drained from my face. "Jordan bit you. If he has something contagious…then you could be infected…"

He sighed. "I know. It's crossed my mind, too. Another reason why I didn't want to come inside of you.

Of course, we've kissed, so that puts you in danger, too." He ran a hand over his face. "I shouldn't have put you in danger. I'm sorry. I wasn't even thinking."

"Ransom, we don't know anything yet. Don't apologize. I would never blame you, anyway. What happened between us was… amazing."

"It was. But… if you get sick, I won't be able to forgive myself."

I clasped his hand. "I won't."

He was silent for a while and then blew out a breath. "You know, my father used to tell me some crazy stories. I thought he was just goofing around, to spook me. I never took them seriously and he didn't really seem to, either. But, what's happening to Jordan… it makes me wonder if there was some actual truth to them."

"What were these stories about?"

"Shifters who couldn't shift and went off the deep-end. Went crazy."

Like Jordan.

"Why couldn't they change?" I asked.

"It was some kind of genetic disease. I think he said it was the same kind of thing that caused vampires to drink blood. So they wouldn't go insane."

"Porphyria?" The word sounded strange. Foreign. Totally out of place in the quiet of the cabin.

He gave me a surprised look. "Yeah. That's it. How did you know?"

"I watched some documentary on the History Channel, or something." A sudden thought hovered at the edge of my mind. Something horrible.

"What?" he asked, noticing the look on my face.

"He's your brother… half-brother. If it's a genetic disease, then you could be affected, too." Images of Ransom, ranting and violent, ran through my mind. Compared to Jordan, he was… huge. If he had the same condition… I couldn't even imagine how terrifying that could be.

"No. I'm fine…if I were like Jordan, I'd know. There'd be signs. I mean, we're about the same age."

"How old are you?"

"Twenty-six."

Ransom was right. They *were* about the same age. Still. He was much bigger. The disease might take longer to show on a larger person.

"But, what if there aren't any? Or, they don't show up until it's too late?"

"There's nothing wrong with me, Hailey," he said firmly. "Speaking of which, I broke Jordan's nose at the diner, right?"

I nodded.

"I'm pretty sure he broke my ribs when he kicked me."

"Okay?"

"The last I checked, his nose was still broken. As for me," Ransom smiled, "I think I pretty much proved that my ribs are healed when you were screaming my name a while ago."

I couldn't help but laugh. "True."

"So, there you go."

Not to mention that Ransom had hurt Jordan pretty badly before he'd taken off.

"So, he's probably off somewhere still licking his wounds as we speak," I said.

"Yeah. He's got some serious injuries, bad enough that it's going to keep him down for a long time."

Something close to relief, sudden and almost overwhelming, flooded through me. "Thank God. I thought for a second that I was going to lose you. I mean, I've barely *had* you," I teased, trying not to cry again. I felt like an emotional wreck in his presence, which normally wasn't the case. But, he seemed to bring out all of my emotions, especially the embarrassing, weak ones.

Ransom's eyes softened. "You're not getting off that easy. I'm here as long as you want me."

"What about what *you* want?" I asked him.

"Hey, I'm exactly where I want to be." He brought my hand to his lips and kissed it. "In bed with you."

I smiled.

His stomach rumbled. "I guess there is another place I want to be," Ransom said with an amused grin. "In front of a plate of food. With you, of course. Are you hungry?"

"Starving."

"I'll check the pantry and see what I can come up with," he said as we thunder rumbled in the distance.

"Okay."

Ransom walked over to the window and looked outside. "Yep. Dark skies are coming."

I stared at his naked torso, admiring his muscles. He looked so damn sexy standing there. "What are we going to do?"

He turned around and walked over to an old chest in the corner. "After we eat?"

"Yeah."

Another rumble of thunder sounded, this time closer. "We wait out the storm and go back tomorrow. To the family."

I frowned. "Your clan?"

"Yeah."

"I doubt, they'll welcome me with open arms after what mine did to yours."

"Don't worry. I'll talk to them. They'll understand that you were just as much of a victim as my father."

I sighed.

"Trust me."

I nodded. He was the only person I actually could trust.

21

Hailey

The rain went on all night, so we ended up staying there until morning. Ransom woke first, and by the time I opened my eyes, he was freshly showered and dressed.

"What time is it?" I asked groggily.

"Still early, but later than I wanted it to be. We need to get going before Jordan shows back up here. You've got time for a shower and a cup of coffee, then we need to hit the road."

The mention of Jordan's name cleared the fog from my head. I climbed out of bed, grabbed a change of clothes, and hit the shower. True to his word, Ransom had a steaming cup of coffee waiting for me.

"Thank you."

"You're welcome," he said, looking out the window. The sun was shining and I could hear birds chirping outside.

I took a sip of my coffee and then turned to pack a few belongings into my duffel. Afterward, I checked my leather satchel, which was still sitting where I'd dropped it. I compulsively opened it, rifling through the contents, and latched it, breathing out a sigh. When I raised my head, I found Ransom looking at me with a curious expression.

"What's in the bag?"

"Bits and pieces of my former life, I guess." I shrugged. "The only pictures I have of my mom and dad.

Old friends. Some letters I received, back before I knew better than to let someone know where I was."

Ransom nodded, then pointed across the room to a small shelf.

"The only pictures I have of my dad." He gave me a smile filled with memories. "Most of them I took when I was a kid, so he's lopsided, or I'd cut off the top of his head." The smile faded. "But they're all I have left of him."

"None of your mother?"

Ransom's eyes dropped and he turned away, looking out the big window.

I winced. Obviously I'd hit a nerve.

"Sorry. I'm being too nosy."

"No. You're fine. The truth is that I never knew her. No one even talked about her much, including my dad. She wasn't part of my life."

I set down the leather satchel and closed the distance between us. I slid my arms around his waist and rested my head against his back. He covered my hands with his, and we stood for a long moment, the quiet of the cabin surrounding us.

"We should go," he murmured a short time later. "Finish your coffee and we'll head back to my motorcycle."

"Okay."

Fifteen minutes later, Ransom led me back down the mountain path. When we came to the spot where Jordan had dragged me, I hesitated.

Ransom turned and looked at me. "What's wrong?"

There was such a feeling of dread in the pit of my stomach. I felt like Jordan was watching and waiting to pounce. Maybe with reinforcements this time. I told Ransom my thoughts.

"He's not here, Hailey. You'd be able to smell him. And stealth isn't his style, you know that."

Ransom was probably right, but it still didn't quell my anxiety. I'd learned long ago not to underestimate Jordan. It was too dangerous.

Nodding, I moved on down the path until we were by the road.

He set his backpack down on the ground. "Wait here. I'll be back."

"Okay," I replied, staring nervously up and down the road.

"You should be safe, but if you see anything at all… unusual, holler."

I nodded.

22

Ransom

I left and made my way through the brush to the motorcycle, which was still safely hidden. When I returned to Hailey, I saw her standing by the side of the road. She was staring down at the skid marks left from Jordan's car, a haunted look on her face. We hadn't talked about what he'd done to her, or the words spoken between them yesterday. As usual, he'd probably terrified the hell out of her. I hoped that in time, she'd offer the information to me herself. I didn't want to push her. She's had enough of that in her life already.

I pulled up on the bike and she got on.

"Ready?" I asked her.

"Yeah."

I turned the Harley around and we headed back to Briar Lake.

Halfway there, we stopped at a rest-stop. Hailey got off first and walked over to the grass. She began stretching and working the kinks out of her back.

"You hungry?" I asked. "We should get something to eat soon."

"Starving."

"Okay." I got off the bike and walked over to her.

Shading her eyes against the sun, she looked at me for a long moment.

"You know, when we get back to Briar Lake… I don't have anywhere else to go. My apartment…" She shrugged. "I'm never going there again."

"You can stay with me."

She frowned. "No. I couldn't ask that off you."

"You don't have to. I'm offering it."

"I shouldn't be your problem. Jordan is going to keep looking for me and you shouldn't have to keep dealing with this bullshit."

"You're definitely not a problem. You're staying with me. Unless, you don't want to."

"It's not that I don't want to. It's just… not fair for you."

I could see it in her eyes that she was grateful for the offer, but Hailey wasn't used to getting help. From anyone

"Look," I put my arms around her waist and stared down into her eyes. "I *want* you to stay with me, okay? In fact, I insist."

She gave me a slow smile. "Insist?"

I nodded. "Yeah. Just… don't make me beg. Especially around Reece. He'll give me shit and never let me live it down."

Hailey chuckled. "Fine. But, just until I figure things out."

"You can stay as long as you want. Speaking of Reece. I'd better call him."

I pulled out my cell and dialed his number. The relief in the older man's voice was clear and I felt a stab of guilt. It hadn't occurred to me that Reece would be so worried and I felt like shit about not calling him back.

"We're on our way back to Briar Lake," I told him. "We should get there around seven."

"Okay. Good. Meet me at the shop when you get here."

"Will do."

After hanging up with Reece, we stopped at a diner, had lunch, and then got back on the road again.

We arrived in Briar Lake a couple hours later, and the storm clouds appeared to be rolling in again.

"Looks like we just made it in time," I said to Hailey, staring up at the sky. "Another storm is coming."

"Yeah."

We drove to the shop and I took the bike around and parked in the alley. After entering through a side-door, we found Reece sitting behind his desk with a half-empty bottle of whiskey in front of him.

"Hey, Ransom. You're a sight for sore eyes. Hailey, I'm glad you're safe." Reece came around from behind the desk and engulfed me in a bear hug.

"Thanks," I replied, hugging him back.

He stepped back and looked at Hailey. After a brief, awkward moment, he pulled her against him in an equally strong embrace. She gave me a surprised look, after he pulled away, and I smiled.

"Sit down." Reese motioned us toward the wooden chairs in front of his desk and then sat back into his own.

He clasped his hands together on the desk and stared at them. "I expect you both have questions. I'm not sure I have any answers that are going to help. Hell, you might just end up more confused by the end of it at all. But, I can tell you what I know… and what I've learned from Malone."

I stared across at him. "Whatever you say has *got* to help. Right now I don't know what's real and what's not. It's been a nightmare. For both of us," I added, looking at Hailey.

"Yeah. I'm sure. I've been dreading this conversation since you called." Reece poured whiskey into a glass and tossed it back. "Honestly, I don't even really know where to start. None of this is easy." His gaze moved to me, and then Hailey, and then he suddenly looked a hundred years older.

"Start with Travis," I said.

He nodded. "You already know that he's a powerful Alpha and that Jordan is your half-brother."

"So, you've said. What about my mother?"

Reece set his elbows on the desk. "You never knew her. None of us did. We knew Drake, though. He was a good guy. So were his clan. He and I used to go hunting and fishing together."

"Wait, so Drake wasn't part of yours?" Hailey asked.

Reece shook his head. "No. Just a good friend."

"Wait, why didn't Ransom's clan raise Ransom after Drake died?" Hailey asked.

He sighed. "They couldn't. They were all killed. By your people."

Hailey's face turned white.

I put my hand over hers. "You obviously weren't involved in that."

She swallowed. "No. I didn't know anything about it."

Reece poured himself another drink, chugged it down, and set the empty glass back onto the desk, staring at it for a while. The next time he spoke, his voice was distant with memories. "When we took you in, you were a hellion, no doubt. Took off as soon as you could, but you always came back."

Frustrated, I leaned forward. He wasn't telling me anything I didn't already know. "Reece. Do you know who killed my father? Or why?"

He looked at me, his tired eyes bloodshot. "I do. I'd hoped I'd never have to tell you any of this, kid. Or who it was." He turned his eyes toward Hailey. "And I'm sorry to be the one to have to say this. To *both* of you. Especially considering everything you've been through together. It's obvious that you've grown close."

Hailey and I stole a glance at each other. She looked just as confused as me. Obviously, we knew Travis was involved. But, bringing her into the picture wasn't making a whole lot of sense at the moment.

He went on. "But so help me, it's the truth." Reece looked directly at Hailey. "It was your father who Travis sent to kill Drake. *And* Ransom."

Hailey made a strangled noise.

I turned and reached for her hand, Reece's words still ringing in my ears. The world suddenly felt unstable, like I'd downed the whiskey, not him.

"So Travis was behind it all? The death of my clan and father?" I asked hoarsely. Although Hailey's old man might have been the one to murder Drake, I wasn't going to hold it against her.

"Yeah, but it's much more than that. See, Travis wanted you dead. Wanted you *out* of the picture. This was even before he knew Jordan was sick."

"So, you know about Jordan's condition?" I asked him.

Reece nodded. "We've heard rumors about it."

I told him what we'd seen.

"It's true then," Reece stated, looking pensive.

I nodded.

"So, Travis knew he was my real father and wanted me dead. Why?" I asked, hating him even more.

"He was afraid. He didn't want you showing up, looking to challenge Jordan as Alpha. The so-called 'accident'…your father's murder… was supposed to include both of you being killed."

Hailey squeezed my hand.

"When it was learned that you didn't die, he went after Drake's clan, systematically, looking for you. He killed them, thinking they were hiding you. But he didn't know you'd come here. That Malone had taken you in."

"So, my father murdered all of these people for Travis?" Hailey asked.

He nodded.

"Why did he kill him then?" she replied.

"He'd failed Travis. Simple as that. Ransom was supposed to die and your father didn't get the job done," Reece said.

"So what about Jordan? Does anyone know exactly what is wrong with him?" Hailey asked. "Or… if it's contagious?"

"The kid's sick, no doubt. We don't know exactly what's causing it. Anyway, from what I heard from Malone, it's the reason behind the whole marriage between the two of you. Get him married. Get you pregnant. Put another Alpha in line. Someone *other* than Ransom. Jordan's not long for this world." He looked at Hailey. "You know better than anyone how crazy he is."

"So I was nothing more than an incubator to carry the next Alpha?" she asked, laughing bitterly. "I guess it shouldn't surprise me."

"Do you really think Jordan has the capacity to love anyone but himself?" I asked her.

"No. I guess not."

"I'll be right back," Reece said, standing up. "I need to use the bathroom."

After he left, Hailey let out a ragged sigh. "So, what now? I'm tired of running… but I don't want to be a burden to you either."

I leaned closer. "You're not a burden and I'm not going to let anything happen to you. Trust me. I'll keep you safe."

I saw a flash of uncertainty in her eyes, but didn't know what else I could say to make her understand just how important she was to me.

"You mean everything to me, Hailey. I know that we've just met, and how hard it is for you to trust people, but I would risk everything to keep you safe. Everything."

Her eyes widened and filled with tears. "I trust you… with my life. And Ransom… I love you."

My world came to an abrupt halt for a heart-stopping moment. Everything I'd heard from Reece, the truth about my father, my history, it all faded. Hailey telling me she loved me, was all that mattered.

"I love you, too, Hailey. With all my heart." I brought her hand to my lips and kissed it. "No more running. We're going to stand our ground and fight this thing together."

"Ransom…" Reece said, standing in the doorway, watching us. "Remember, you're still a wanted man. A threat. To Jordan *and* to Travis himself. You're in more danger than anyone at the moment. Especially since Jordan's disease is progressing the way you say it is."

"This is bullshit. I don't want to be Alpha to their clan. Never will."

Reece nodded, his face drawn tight. "That doesn't matter. They're going to come after you… especially since you're involved with her." He jerked his head toward Hailey. "You're a marked man."

"Looks like I always was. Nothing has changed," I replied. "Only that the two of us are fighting this battle together now."

"Wrong. It's more than two. You have me and the others," Reece said. "We've got your back. Always have. Just don't take off like that again. We can't help you if we don't know where you're at."

I nodded and stood up. "Thanks, man. I don't know what I'd do without you."

Reece hugged me again. "You're family. You don't have to do worry about going it alone. Neither of you," he said to Hailey.

"Thank you," she said softly.

Reece nodded.

23

Hailey

"It's not much, but I call it home," Ransom said as he held the door for me. We were on the second floor of an older brick apartment building. One that wasn't much different than my own.

I glanced nervously back down the hallway one last time before stepping inside of his apartment. I was both relieved and apprehensive about being there. I didn't think it would take much for Jordan to find out where Ransom lived.

I set my duffel bag near the door. Behind me I heard the click of the lock, followed by the sound of the deadbolt.

"This looks perfectly fine to me. Anyway, I'm so tired right now, I can barely see straight," I replied, staring at his living room, which was slightly bigger than my own. The kitchen was blocked off by a wall, but there was a small dining room with an old dinette table near a window. Straight ahead, and down the hall, were two doors, one with a bed visible through the crack. The other I assumed to be the bathroom. The place was a little messy, with books set on almost every surface. But, it smelled clean and looked homey.

Ransom dropped his backpack onto an old, beat-up brown recliner. "Tell me about it. It's been a hell of a ride, hasn't it?"

I nodded. In the corner of the room, a battered electric guitar leaned against the wall. I gestured toward it. "That yours?"

"Yeah"

"Are you in a band?"

"Kind of. I get together with some of the guys at the shop and we play sometimes. Typical garage band stuff. Nothing fancy. But, we do okay." He gave a dismissive wave of his hand before turning away. There was more than a hint of pride in his voice, which made me believe that he might be really good.

"That's pretty cool. You'll have to play for me sometime."

"For sure. Are you hungry?"

"Yeah."

"Okay. I'll see what I can whip up." He headed toward the kitchen.

"Need any help?" I dropped onto the couch and kicked off my shoes.

"Nah. Just relax."

My eyelids felt heavy and I was relieved that he wanted to take care of it himself. I wasn't much of a cook, anyway. But, he'd been taking such good care of me and I knew it wasn't really fair for him to do all the work. "You sure? I can help, you know."

"I know. You can make the next meal."

"No problem."

I listened to the comforting sounds of Ransom rattling drawers and banging cupboard doors, and leaned my head back. I closed my eyes and let out a sigh. It was a relief to be off the road and somewhere safe, at least for the moment. But, even so, my thoughts refused to stop spinning as my mind replayed everything that had brought us to that point. So much had happened. So much had changed. Both of our worlds had been turned upside down in more ways than one. It seemed almost impossible that we'd just met. He was practically still a stranger, more unknown than known. But, I trusted him with my life and so far, he'd done a damn fine job of keeping me safe.

"So, what are we going to do about Jordan and Travis?" I asked, feeling anxious again. Although Ransom's clan was close, we were alone and vulnerable. If we were both marked, and if Travis was desperate enough, I knew it was only a matter of time before someone showed up on Ransom's doorstep.

I opened my eyes. Ransom appeared in the kitchen doorway, a knife in one hand, a jar of mustard in the other. "We eat. We rest. We don't panic."

I smiled grimly. "I just don't know how you can be so calm right now."

"I'm not going to let them get to me, that's how. Neither should you."

I knew that he'd mentioned not wanting to be Alpha to any clan, but from where I was sitting, Ransom seemed to have the qualities that could make him a good one. He was level-headed. Strong. Brave. Even after finding out about his father, he'd not let it beat him down. He'd risen above it, demanding answers. Not pity.

"I'm... not as strong as you are."

"The hell you're not. You left a bad situation and never looked back. You walked away from your Alpha. You've survived on your own, Hailey. And you're only twenty-one?"

"Almost twenty-two."

He nodded. "Exactly. Still very young. You should be proud of yourself. You didn't cower and give in to those bastards. You got the hell out of there and never looked back."

I let out a shaky sigh. He was right. Maybe I shouldn't be so hard on myself. I wasn't just running from Jordan. I was hiding from my entire pack. There was strength in numbers and I'd been alone. Standing my ground wouldn't have helped me any. It would have gotten me married by now and, more than likely, a mother.

"You just need some food and some rest. We both do," he said when I didn't answer.

"Yeah, you might be right," I replied.

"I'm making ham sandwiches. Do you like pickles?"

"Yeah and that sounds great."

"Good. The fridge is pretty bare, so it's all I have right now. We'll go grocery shopping soon and pick up some more things."

"Okay."

We ate our sandwiches in silence, and when we were finished, Ransom cleared the dishes and then held out his hand to me. "Come on. You look exhausted. Let's get some rest."

I stood up and he led me to the bedroom. Ransom turned on the light and glanced around the room after we entered. He gave me an embarrassed smile. "Sorry. Guess I'll have to fire the cleaning lady."

The queen-sized bed was rumpled, and there were a few pieces of clothing on the floor, and more books lying around. But, the room was cool, clean, and smelled like him. As far as I was concerned, it was damn inviting.

"Seriously, it looks great."

He walked over to me. "It'll look even greater with you naked and in my bed," Ransom murmured, putting his arms around my waist and pulling me against him.

"I guess you're not as tired as I thought you were."

"Believe me, I'm exhausted. I'm also hornier than hell. You have that effect on me."

I could feel his hard-on pressing against my pelvis. It was making my sex twitch in response.

"We don't have to fool around, though. We can just get some rest for now," he added.

I yawned. "Honestly, I don't think I could sleep if I wanted to."

"Why not?"

I looked pensively toward his bedroom window. "Because he's out there. *They* are out there. Somewhere."

Ransom sighed. "You have nothing to worry about. Before we left his shop, Reece said he'd send a couple of the clan members over, to keep an eye on my building. They're going to rotate for the next couple of days, or until we know we're safe."

I frowned. With Jordan on the loose, I'd never be safe, nor him. Even if Travis reeled Jordan back home, something told me that at this point, he wouldn't listen. He wanted to destroy both of us and I knew he wouldn't stop until he had his way.

"It'll be okay, Hailey. Trust me. We'll get Jordan taken care of, one way or another," Ransom said, as if reading my mind.

"I do trust you. It's just… I've been running for so long. It's the only thing that's kept me safe, besides you. Sitting still and knowing that he's out there, hell, maybe even in town… it just feels wrong."

"I know, but it's all we can do right now. Anyway, Reece is going to ask Malone to make some calls. He's hoping he might talk some sense into Travis. Maybe he can talk him into calling Jordan off."

"Why would he do that, though? If he wants you dead and me pregnant with his grandson?"

"I don't know. Maybe Malone will threaten him? He's pretty damn intimidating."

I sighed. Nobody scared Travis. Not even Malone. I'd heard him talk shit about Ransom's pack and how he thought they were weak. It was a waste of time.

Ransom gave me a reassuring smile. "You're safe here. We both are. Let's take advantage of it."

I wasn't so sure, but at least his pack was outside keeping an eye on things. "Okay."

"In fact… the only screams we have to worry about are the ones you're going to be making when you're in my bed," Ransom said, his eyes turning dark with desire.

I smiled. "Oh, yeah?"

"Oh, yeah." His fingers slid beneath the thin cotton of my shirt and were warm against my skin. My exhaustion faded a little, replaced with an anticipatory tingle of arousal.

He bent his head and his mouth found mine. His lips were warm, and what started off as a light kiss soon grew powerful and primal. A now-familiar thud of arousal hit me in the mid-section, and I moaned against his mouth.

I suddenly wanted him. Almost desperately.

Caught up in my desires, I tore at his T-shirt, ripping the fabric and pulling it away from his taut chest.

Ransom broke away from me with a gasp. "Not tired anymore?" His eyes bored into mine, their depths matching the heat that raged inside of me.

"Less talk, more action," I replied breathlessly.

Ransom smiled. He grabbed the front of my shirt, mimicking my actions and tearing the fabric. Shoving it aside, he ran his hands over my bra and then crushed my breasts together. Groaning in the back of his throat, he slid my bra under my nipples and then cupped my breasts in his hands. I closed my eyes as he brought his hot mouth down and began licking and sucking one tip and then the other.

Shivers of pleasure raced through me. I ran my fingers through his hair, pulling at it as his mouth became more aggressive.

"You're so beautiful," he growled against my breasts. Then, in one movement, he tore the bra down the center, freeing them. He gripped my breasts, squeezing and kneading the soft flesh almost painfully. The primal need inside of me grew as did the wetness between my legs. I pulled Ransom's head back down to my nipples and moaned as his lips returned to them. On fire, I reached down to his zipper and felt his desire. Now, panting and desperate, I tugged at the button and unzipped his jeans, freeing his hard-on. Wrapping my hand around the shaft, I squeezed the length, aching to feel it inside of me.

Groaning, Ransom slid his hand over my ass and then between my legs, stoking the fire already there.

I reached down, unbuttoned and unzipped my jeans. He pushed them down below my hips and then dropped to his knees. He pulled my panties and jeans down to the floor in one movement, and I kicked them away.

Ransom slid his hands up my thighs, cupped my ass, and pulled me forward. He buried his face against my stomach, his tongue flicking a circle around my navel.

My fingers found his hair again, winding into the thick strands. Trembling with desire, my legs began to shake as he kissed a line over the curve of my stomach and headed south.

His hands moved to the insides of my thighs, pushing them apart, giving him access to my womanhood. I gasped in pleasure as he buried his face between my legs and began licking my folds. Soon, he had me mewling and whimpering as his tongue danced and strummed me like the guitar in his living room. He added his fingers and the pleasure almost became almost too much. The sensations Ransom created spiraled upward until I was peaking in an explosion of ecstasy. I threw my head back and screamed while my body shuddered in Ransom's strong grip. When I was finally able to catch my breath, I looked down at him.

"Take me, Ransom. Now… please."

He stood up and leaned me down over the bed. Ransom spread my legs, twirled the head of his cock around my wet heat, and then plunged into me. Groaning, he pulled out halfway and then filled me again.

"You're so tight," he growled, placing a hand on my lower back as he picked up speed.

I cried out, rocking forward from the force of his thrusts while holding onto the side of the bed. His weight and strength, the power of his thrusts, pushed me down to my elbows. It felt so good, especially at the angle he was. His movements grew harder and faster, his breathing harsh.

"Ransom," I moaned. "It feels so good."

The pain and heat, the power of the man who controlled my body, it all came crashing together. I arched and threw my head back as everything broke loose, engulfing me in a powerful orgasm.

Ransom's cries rose almost as loud as mine, as he buried himself inside of me. His fingers dug into my hips, pulling me back against his and I could feel his body straining against mine. Finally, when it seemed he couldn't possibly fill me any more than he already had, he came.

I fell forward then, twisting beneath Ransom to look back at him over my shoulder. The last vestiges of my orgasm swirled through me as I watched him finish his. I could feel him throbbing in time with the deep pulsing of my own body.

Finally, he fell forward onto the bed beside me. He was still breathing hard and there was a sheen of sweat covering his chest. I curled against him, knowing that there was no place in life I wanted to be but there. With the man who not only owned my heart, but my body and soul.

"Ransom."

"Yeah?"

I snuggled closer to him. "I love you."

"I love you, too, Hailey. More than anything."

Smiling to myself, I closed my eyes and let the exhaustion take over. Moments later, I was fast asleep.

24

Ransom

My eyes sprung open in the dark. A subtle noise had woken me, followed by a soft knocking at the door.

I looked at Hailey, who was still sleeping soundly. A smile ghosted my lips, fading as I climbed out of bed, trying hard not to disturb her. I pulled on a pair of black sweatpants and crept out of the bedroom.

The living room was dark, but I left the light off. Even in human form, I could see everything clearly and smell the person knocking on my door. It was Marco, one of the clan members. If he was on the other side of the door, chances were he wasn't bringing good news.

I opened the door.

Marco stood in the hallway. His eyes were wild and his compact body thrummed with excitement. The truth was, he was always tense and easily excitable but basically a good guy. It was clear something had him agitated more than usual tonight.

"What is it?" I moved into the hallway, shutting the door behind me.

"Someone picked up Jordan's scent." Marco said in a low voice.

"Where?"

"A couple blocks from here."

"You sure it's him?"

Marco snorted a laugh. "No doubt it's him. The guy smells like death. Reece said he was sick, but this is worse than anything I've ever smelled. He's not contagious, is he?"

I shook my head. "Not unless being an asshole is contagious. We think it might be some hereditary thing. Not something you need to worry about."

Me, on the other hand... time would only tell.

Marco looked relieved.

The metal door slamming shut at the bottom of the stairs was deafening in the quiet hallway.

"Ransom needs to know," one of the voices said. "He could be here any minute."

Marco tensed up.

I ran past him, my bare feet pounding as I raced downstairs. Three of our clan brothers were at the bottom, all of them now talking at once.

One of them, a tall, thin guy named Bruce, looked up at me as I reached the landing above them. "It's Jordan. He's getting closer."

"Is he alone?" I asked, walking down to meet them.

"It looks that way," Bruce replied.

My pulse began to race. This was it, then. My chance to finish this thing with Jordan. Our code of honor dictated that the fight would just be between the two of us, but with the backing of my clan, I definitely had an advantage.

I was almost out the door when I heard a door open from above. I knew instinctively that it was Hailey. I raced back upstairs and met her at the top. She was dressed in one of my T-shirts. Her eyes were wide with fear and her face was drawn. "Is it Jordan?"

"Yes. Stay in the apartment." I looked at Marco, who'd followed me back. "Keep an eye on her, will you?"

Marco nodded.

"Screw that. I'm coming with you," she said firmly.

Before I could answer, she disappeared down the hallway, heading back to my apartment.

I sighed. I wanted her safe and didn't have the time to fight with her.

"Marco, stay with her. Don't let her out of your sight. Jordan is hell-bent on getting his paws on her and will do whatever it takes. He took her once, and I'm not letting that happen again."

Marco nodded again and headed after her.

As I went back downstairs, I could hear Hailey arguing with Marco. The guy was going to have his hands full. I just hoped he could keep her out of the middle of whatever the hell was going to break loose outside.

I burst through the door into the parking lot. The moon was low and the clouds surrounding it gave it a feeble silvery light. The parking lot was mostly deserted and only a few cars huddled near the street.

Standing in a rough circle on the asphalt, were my clan mates. Some of them I knew by name. Some only by face. Most of the time I'd catch brief glimpses of them as they dropped off or picked up bikes for Malone, who owned the shop. I was shocked to see most of them there. And grateful as hell.

As I approached, they turned to me with expectant looks. For a moment I felt almost disconnected and unsure of how to approach a bunch of guys ready to risk their lives like this.

They're family, I reminded myself.

Just like Reece had been trying to beat through my thick skull since he'd taken me in.

Family took care of family.

And that was what these clan members were there for. To stand behind me and help protect Hailey.

My brothers.

A rush of emotions filled me as I stepped closer. For the first time, I really felt connected to the pack. They were loyal and I would forever reciprocate.

One of them approached me, slightly out of breath. His name was Roger. "He's close, real close."

I lifted my head and sniffed the air. Jordan's scent reached me quickly. It was pungent and foul, filled with sickness and rot.

I shook my head, wanting to clear the scent from my nose. It was near impossible.

"He smells like he's dying. What's going on with him?" Roger asked.

"He has some kind of genetic affliction that's causing him to go crazy," I said. "He can't control when he shifts, either. He doesn't always change completely. So don't be thrown by that."

There was a crash at the end of the alley that ran alongside the building. A garbage can came hurtling toward us out of the darkness. Everyone scattered, melting into the shadows.

I moved back toward my apartment building and Hailey stepped outside, still wearing my shirt along with a pair of jeans. Marco was behind her, shaking his head.

"Sorry, man. I tried talking her out of coming, but… she's stubborn as hell."

"Yeah. I know. Get out of the light. Jordan is close," I replied.

They moved next to me, into the shadows.

"You're not making things easier," I murmured to Hailey.

"Look, I'm not staying up there alone." Her voice was an agitated whisper in the darkness.

"You weren't alone… but this isn't the time for an argument," I muttered.

"I know. I can smell him," she replied.

My gaze swept the dim lot, listening and waiting for Jordan to show himself. And then it came, the gritty sound of footsteps in the alley.

I looked at Marco and Hailey and nodded.

It was him.

From the sound of claws hitting pavement, it was obvious that Jordan was walking on all fours.

"Marco, go find the others. Tell them he's mine, though. You're only here to protect Hailey. I'm taking care of Jordan once and for all."

Marco nodded and slipped away into the darkness.

"Hailey…" I turned back to her, and to my amazement, she was stripping off her clothes. "Stop, Hailey. It's not your fight."

"It's always been my fight," she growled.

For a minute, everything else faded as I watched Hailey begin the transformation. She seemed to shimmer in the dim moonlight, dropping gracefully from her human form to land on four paws as a glorious white Lycan. She was nothing short of beautiful. Her lush female curves translated into a sleekly muscled beast covered in soft, white fur.

She looked up at me, her eyes flashing.

"Damn," I whispered in approval.

Her head snapped up and the hackles rose on her back. I tensed up.

Hailey's nostrils flared, and at that instant, I caught a strong wave of Jordan's scent.

Hailey growled low, warning me.

The power of my beast rose up inside. I loved this moment and how the inner force swelled, threatening to consume me. It was almost overwhelming in its intensity. The experience bordered on erotic, the same feeling I had on the edge of an orgasm. But instead of letting go and surrendering, at the last moment, I fought to gain control of all that chaotic energy. I mastered the wildness, harnessed the power, and channeled it into my Lycan form.

Dropping to the asphalt on all fours, I headed away from the building, Hailey following behind me. Ahead, spreading across the parking lot in silent unison was my clan, their dark canine forms still in the shadows.

"I see you brought friends to the party, Ransom. Too afraid to fight me by yourself?" Jordan's words were human, but his voice sounded like a hoarse growl.

The others leaped out of the shadows and surrounded Hailey. When I saw that she was safe, I turned just as Jordan emerged from the alley.

The last time I'd seen Jordan, he'd been a mess. The form emerging now was even worse. Hardly recognizable. His head and ears were misshapen, his eyes were bloodshot, and a row of fangs jutted out from a human jaw. His snout appeared to also be caught in limbo, which made me wonder if he could even breathe properly. As for the rest of him, thick fur clumped in matted forms on his face and neck, his limbs bowed, and his wounds appeared to be healing, but at a very slow rate.

The others, having not seen Jordan's state, stared in shock as he moved closer.

"Pathetic coward," Jordan scoffed in his strange, garbled voice. "You had to bring an army to fight your battle? You're a disgrace to our kind."

I growled and then charged forward.

Jordan laughed, a high, sick sound that grated on my nerves, before lunging forward.

I met him full force, diving beneath Jordan's belly. I could smell his foul, hot breath and heard the clash of his teeth as he nipped my neck. We rolled across the pavement, neither of us getting a grip on the other. We broke apart and I scrambled to my feet, turning quickly to face him again.

For an instant, Jordan's face held two forms: Lycan competing with human. I watched as his lower jaw extended. I heard the bones crack and break, as it reformed into a canine's muzzle. Just before the process was completed, however, the shift stopped, leaving him even more malformed and hideous than before.

Then, it hit me like the proverbial ton of bricks. I needed to strike when he was between forms. When he was distracted. After our last rumble, I needed every advantage. I needed to beat him without help from the others, too. This was between us and us alone.

Determined to get this over with, I circled Jordan, drawing him into the feeble circle of light cast by the lone street light. He moved with me, nails clicking on the asphalt, eyes locked on mine.

Jordan stopped suddenly and shook his head briskly. He threw his head back, howled at the sky, and then rose on his hind legs. I watched as his forelegs shifted back to arms and paws changed to hands. Whatever had a hold on him, it was running wild with his ability to keep any form. If I hadn't despised him so much, I would have almost felt sorry for the asshole. But, I didn't.

I charged, hitting Jordan in his stomach and knocking him backward onto the pavement. I landed on his chest and his hands closed around my neck. This time his grip was weak. Incompetent. Frustrated, he cried out as his fingers shrank and morphed back into paws, clawing ineffectually at my neck. Eventually, he lost his grip and I pressed forward, sinking my fangs into Jordan's neck. A rush of blood filled my mouth. A hot, foul-tasting liquid. I gagged, but held on, desperately wanting to let go and get the horrid taste out of my mouth.

Jordan kicked at me with his back legs, his sharp claws scraping at my underbelly. Horrendous pain flared in my gut and I knew he was doing some major damage. But, I held on, twisting my head and tearing at his flesh with my teeth.

Suddenly, he twisted and struggled beneath me, his legs no longer kicking me in the stomach or clawing at my hide. Relieved, I let go of his neck and spit the diseased blood onto the ground.

Jordan let out an angry cry.

Confused, I turned to find one of my clan mates tugging on Jordan's leg. It was Pete.

Jordan became incensed. He pushed up hard against me with enough force that I went flying.

Shocked at his strength, I jumped back on all fours and watched him kick Pete in the jaws. The sickening crack of breaking bone echoed in the parking lot. Pete yelped, a high whistling sound of pain before scuttling backward, away from him. His jaw hung askew as he slunk back into the shadows with the others.

Several more Lycan began to advance, but I called them off.

"You think you can defeat me?" Jordan sneered, standing on his hind legs again, looking almost terrifying. "Look at what I did to your friend. The others know how powerful I am. They're all pissing themselves with fear because they know I'm an Alpha." He glared down the line at all of us. "I'm stronger than every one of you pussies."

I growled at him.

"Come on, Ransom, is that all you got?" Jordan's face began to shift again. He dropped to the ground, wavering between Lycan and human. For a long moment, we stared at each other. His bloodshot eyes were wild and heated by whatever internal hellfire raged inside of him.

His lips pulled back into a tight grin. "You know, even Hailey puts up more of a fight than you. Speaking of… I'd better collect what's mine as long as the bitch is here."

Catching me off guard, Jordan lunged to my right, sliding past me.

I whirled to snap at his fur but caught only air. I watched as he leaped over the line of Lycan guarding Hailey. Marco, who stood next to her, charged, but Jordan knocked him away as if he was nothing more than a pesky fly. The force was so strong, that when Marco hit the ground his head crashed against the concrete, knocking him out.

Was his affliction making him stronger?

Jordan smiled evilly at Hailey. "Hello, baby. Miss me?"

The others sprang at Jordan and I watched as he took them out, one-by-one, indicating that he was definitely, somehow, getting stronger.

Hailey stood frozen in shock, watching as he fought them off. Torn between wanting to jump in and helping her, I howled and got her attention. She crouched down and was about to spring toward me when Jordan batted one of the other Lycan away and pounced. He slammed her against the dumpster and she fell into a crumpled heap.

"This is all your fault," he growled down at her. "Their blood will be on your hands."

Enraged, I pushed off the concrete and hit Jordan hard in the mid-section. He fell away from Hailey, tumbling sideways. I quickly slammed my body against him again with as much force as I could muster. This time, I felt ribs breaking beneath me. I sank my teeth into Jordan's shoulder and came away with a mouthful of dirty, bloody, matted fur. Spitting it out, I padded over to Hailey and nudged her softly. She opened her eyes, to my relief.

"Bastard... fucking bastard." he rasped, pulling himself along the ground with his bloody hands. The upper half of his body was shifting again and his nails began to rip from the fingertips as he crawled.

Two Lycan came to Hailey's aid, giving me a chance to follow Jordan. I moved warily toward him as he turned fully back into human form. Grunting and mumbling to himself, he slowly got back to his feet and swayed. He was bleeding from his ear to his neck, the blood running, but not gushing. Unfortunately, I'd missed the major arteries. He held his side, which appeared black-and-blue, however. It looked like he might have been bleeding internally, which had to hurt like hell.

Jordan spat a foamy glob of spit onto the pavement. He wiped his mouth on the back of his hand. "You think you got me?" The words were clotted in his throat. He spat another wad of blood. "You pathetic fuck."

I growled at him.

"Come on, *brother.*" Jordan held his ground. "Let's see what else you got."

With a fierce howl, I dove, hitting him at the knees and driving him back into the metal fence that ran behind the dumpster. He slammed into it and then collapsed down onto the pavement, moaning. From where I was standing, he appeared to be weakening, although for how long, I didn't know.

"So, tell me, Ransom… what was it like fucking the bitch? Were you even man enough to get it up?"

I was torn between wanting to change back into my human form so I could beat him with my bare fists, or tear out his jugular with my canines. That was when I remembered another story my father had told me. He'd called it a legend.

"There was once a Lycan who could control his changes so well, that he could stop mid-process. He could walk as a man and still feast as a beast. He didn't have to be one or the other. He could be both."

"Did he also have the disease, Papa?" I'd asked, intrigued.

He'd looked at me hard and with worry. *"No, but his genes might have caused the disease."*

In that instant, it had seemed like he'd wanted to tell me more but hadn't. It had almost been as if he'd been too afraid to.

Something inside of me clicked. A deep awakening.

I backed up and began to change back to my human form. This time, however, I put all of my strength into halting it midway. It was painful. Almost excruciating. I could hear the blood rushing through me and the sound of bones shifting and moving. Suddenly, however, the pain ceased, as did the movement under my skin. I opened my eyes and saw Jordan staring at me in shock and then anger.

"No," he growled.

I looked down at myself in astonishment.

It had worked. Successfully. I was part canine. Part human. And it felt glorious.

My legs were thick, heavy, and lined with fur. But they were as long as my human ones. My hands had fur and claws, but no paws. My junk? Well, that was an entirely different story… Let's just say it was impressive in its own right.

"How are you able to control it?" Jordan demanded as I stood up on my hind legs.

Not knowing if I could speak, I opened my mouth and rasped "I'm just better than you," I goaded.

He glared at me. "Bullshit."

I didn't care what he thought. I felt strong and my head was clear. It was invigorating. My excitement… almost orgasmic. I glanced at Hailey, who looked frightened and worried.

"I'm fine," I told her.

Her eyes traveled down to my jutting penis, which was expressing my excitement. Had I been wholly human, I might have been a little embarrassed. But the dog in my stood there proudly, showing it off.

Jordan laughed coldly. "Enjoy it now. You'll soon be in such pain, you'll wish for death. Beg for it."

My cock deflated. What if he was right? "Did you ever have control?"

He didn't answer. Just kept smiling like a madman.

My clan brothers stepped warily closer. I gave them what I hoped was a reassuring smile as well.

"This means nothing. You will never be Alpha," Jordan growled.

I looked at him. "I never wanted to be."

"Liar." He grabbed something from the ground, a crushed beer can, and sprang at me.

I caught him by throat, knocked it from his hand, and raised him high into the air. He seemed so light. My newfound strength seemed to have tripled in the state I was currently in. It was exhilarating. "You just can't leave well enough alone, can you?"

Jordan's eyes seemed to bug out of his head as he stared at me in terror. "Wait."

I glared at him. I could tell that he was desperately trying to shift, but it wasn't working. I knew if I didn't finish him off, this war between the three of us would never end.

"You brought this onto yourself," I reminded him.

He glared at me.

I brought him back down to the ground and went for the jugular, tearing it out. Blood sprayed everywhere, dripping down my muzzle and all over the both of us.

Shrieking, Jordan tried beating my shoulders, his strength still powerful even now as the blood drained from his neck. But, no match for mine. Not anymore.

The pounding on my shoulders grew weaker as I bored down, sinking my jaws deeper into his neck. Finally, he let go of my fur and his hands fell away. I released him and watched as he dropped to the ground. His eyes stared blankly into the night sky.

It was over.

Finally.

Relieved, I let out a ragged breath and that was when something brushed my thigh.

Hailey.

I bent down and pulled her into my arms.

She nuzzled my neck and I closed my eyes, thankful she was alive and relatively unharmed.

Sirens in the distance startled us. I stood up and was met by stares from the clan, even Marco, who was standing unsteadily, but standing. I felt something from them that hadn't been there before. A new kind of respect. Or, maybe it was fear. Whatever it was, I didn't exactly mind it.

I waved at them to go and they took off.

Hailey and I hurried into the building and made it back to my apartment.

25

Hailey

The clan was gone, having melted back into the streets to wherever they'd come from. Hearing the sirens, I quickly followed Ransom back into his apartment. He closed the door and the reassuring sound of the locks engaging sent a mixture of both relief and uncertainty through me. Although it was over, I was still a wreck.

Somehow sensing my fears, he pulled me against his chest, and I melted against him. For a long time, we stood silently in the dark room, holding each other and listening to the sirens outside.

"What if they find us?" I whispered.

"The police?"

I'd meant my old clan, but I was worried about both. I nodded.

"Nobody will be able to identify us," he said, reassuring me. "Hell, if there were witnesses who saw anything, the cops will think they're on drugs anyway, right?"

"True."

The sirens eventually faded, and Ransom peeked outside, down toward the parking lot.

"How many are down there?" I asked, walking over to the window.

"Three squads," he replied, letting go of the blinds. He turned around and faced me. "We need to shower."

He was right. We were both a bloody mess. Fortunately, my wounds were already healing, and from what I could tell of Ransom, he seemed to be in pretty good shape as well.

I followed him into the bathroom and we took a quick hot one together. I could tell he wanted to do more, but my mind was preoccupied with everything that had happened. Being the gentleman he was, and sensing my mood, Ransom kept his hands to himself.

"Are you okay?" he asked as we were drying off.

Images of him ripping Jordan's throat raced through my head. I couldn't believe he was actually dead. I'd been afraid of him for so long. Had been *running* from him for so long. I knew I was safe now, at least from Jordan. And yet… I still felt anxious.

"You're safe…" Ransom said when I didn't answer.

I forced a smile to my face. "I know. It's just so hard to believe he's really gone. I keep expecting him to come crashing through the doorway."

Ransom pulled me against him. "He can't hurt you anymore."

"I know… it's just…" my voice trailed off.

"I get it. It's a big change in your life, it's going to take some time to adjust."

I rested my head against his chest. "As long as we're together, I can get through anything. But yeah, not having to sleep with one eye open is going to take some getting used to."

"I'm sure."

After a few seconds, he released me and we headed back into his bedroom. Before getting into bed, he walked over to the window and peeked outside again.

"What's happening?" I asked.

"Just what you'd expect. More cops and now an ambulance."

I shuddered. "He's dead though, right?"

"Oh, hell yeah." He released the blinds and walked over to the bed. "Not even Jordan can come back from that."

Swallowing, I got into the bed and he joined me. He pulled me into his arms and we both closed our eyes. We lay there quietly for a long time and I knew he wasn't asleep. One question in particular was nagging me and it seemed as good a time as any to ask.

"Why did you run off with me in the first place and take me to your cabin?"

"I was hoping we'd end up here," he said with a smile in his voice.

"Seriously, Ransom. You could have faced Jordan then, or left me there. But you left everything, without a second thought."

Ransom shifted beneath me. "You're not the only one who runs from things. I've been running away most of my life." His voice was low. "Difference is; I wasn't running away from someone. Well, I was, but I thought I was running toward something… something better. Greener grass, and all that."

"But you always come back to your clan?"

"Yeah. Like a bad penny. And they always take me back." He was quiet for a long moment and I knew he was deep in thought.

"You know; I don't even know some of those guys who showed up here tonight," he continued. "Not by name, not by face. A few I'd only seen at Reece's shop. I had never talked to any of them. But they came here to help me… help *us*."

"I'm so grateful for that," I replied softly.

"Me, too. But, I guess that's what family does. Stands by you even if they don't know you. And you're part of that now, too."

His words put me more at ease. "So we're both done running. I want to believe it, but it's hard."

"I know. We just have to take one day at a time."

"Yeah."

He yawned. "We should get some sleep." He kissed me on the lips and then became quiet again.

As exhausted as I was, sleep still eluded me. My mind just wouldn't stop circling around everything that had happened. It kept playing over every detail… from the first day I'd met Ransom at the diner, to Jordan showing up at and raising hell. Then me dragging Ransom into my crazy life. Not to mention Jordan finding us, kidnapping me, and Ransom chasing us down.

My heart swelled.

I'd been a total stranger to him but he'd risked his life for me. If it had been anyone else, I knew that I'd be dead right now. Ransom entering my life had been nothing short of a miracle.

I smiled to myself. Somewhere in all of the craziness, we'd fallen in love. Deeply. Out of chaos had come something pure. Good. Loving. It seemed almost too good to be true.

Was it?

I closed my eyes for what seemed like the hundredth time, drew a deep breath, and finally felt myself drift off into a deep sleep.

26

Hailey

The rumble of voices dragged me from my slumber. I opened my eyes and saw that the room was filled with soft sunlight. I tried to focus on the clock by the bed, pulling it toward me. My eyes widened in shock. I was late afternoon, almost evening. I'd been asleep for over twelve hours.

Voices came steadily from the living room. Among them, I recognized Ransom's… and then Reece's. Someone else was with them as well. None of the words were clear, but the tone was. I was pretty sure they were talking about Jordan. About me. About the mess that was my life. The mess that was now Ransom's, too.

Climbing quietly out of bed, I pulled on my jeans and T-shirt. I then slipped to the door and peeked out of the bedroom. Ransom and Reece, along with a third man, sat around the kitchen table. The tension between them was almost visible. Combined with the testosterone level in the room, I was definitely out of my element.

"It's not that simple, Ransom," the stranger said. "You think you've gotten rid of the problem by getting rid of Jordan, but there's more to this than just him. You're in hot water."

I frowned as I stared at the man speaking. He was muscular and dressed in jeans and a polo shirt. He reminded me of military, with his brush-cut salt-and-pepper hair and commanding tone.

Their Alpha.

Ransom shook his head. "There's nothing left to talk about. Hailey's problem—our problem—was Jordan. He attacked us, unprovoked, and I gave him several chances to walk away. But, he wouldn't. Now he's paid the price and no longer anyone's problem."

Reece sat forward, resting his arms on the table. "Stop being such a bullhead, Ransom. Listen to us. You killed the son of one of the most powerful Alphas around. Travis's not just going to let you have a free pass on that."

"There are ramifications here, big ones. Things you're not paying attention to." The stranger frowned. "You think this is just about Jordan and Hailey, but it's not. Now it's about you."

Ransom sat back, arms folded across his chest, a dark scowl on his face. He looked up and caught sight of me. The scowl faded and he relaxed. "Hailey."

Reece and the other man turned around to look at me. I stood frozen, feeling almost like an intruder.

Ransom got up and walked over to me. He took my hand and led me over to the table.

"I'm glad you're awake. This is as much about you now as it is about me," he said.

I forced a smile to my face.

He pulled up another chair for me and I sat down. Ransom moved back to his seat and dropped heavily onto it.

"This is Malone." He nodded toward the third man. "My... I guess, *our*, Alpha. Malone, this is Hailey."

"Pleasure to meet you, Hailey." Malone rose slightly and extended his hand across the small table. I shook it. His grip was firm and his hand warm. He met my gaze squarely. "I wish it was under better circumstances."

"Me, too."

He released my hand, sitting back but keeping his eyes on me. They were dark brown, almost black, as he took in every detail of my face. It felt like he was trying to read my mind or deciding exactly what to do with me.

Pulling my knees up, I settled my feet on the chair and wrapped my arms around my legs. I was suddenly self-conscious, feeling exposed. Almost as if I was sitting naked in front of the man. The moment seemed to stretch on forever. Then, Malone turned back to Ransom.

"Travis contacted me. He wants to meet you," he said to him.

"Meet with him? Not particularly thrilled with that idea," he replied dryly.

Malone reached out, resting his hand on Ransom's shoulder. "I know. Don't worry, I won't let you go alone. I'll go with you."

I raised my head. "I'm going, too." The words came out a hell of a lot louder than I'd wanted. I coughed and tried again. "I'm going with Ransom."

"No, you're not." Malone stared at me. His gaze was hard, and a shiver ran down my spine. "This isn't your problem anymore, Hailey."

I set my feet on the floor and sat up straight, meeting Malone's eyes. As brave as I wanted to be, my heart was doing a jittery beat in my chest. "But I'm the one who got Ransom involved in this. I'm *not* letting him do this alone, just like he didn't let me deal with Jordan alone. We're a package deal now."

Malone held my gaze, eyes going hard as granite. I wanted to look down and break away from his piercing look, but I lifted my chin instead.

An electric current passed between us. An unspoken challenge. It took all of my nerve to not drop my eyes. Finally, Malone shrugged, eyes narrowing. The granite look was still there, but the challenge had faded. I almost thought I saw a begrudging look of approval pass over his face.

"Fine. It's clear you're as stubborn as he is." He turned to Ransom, jerking his thumb in my direction. "It looks like you found someone as bullheaded as you, Ransom."

There was a muffled laugh from Reece, which drew a scowl from both Ransom, and Malone.

Malone sighed and ran his hand across his face. "We meet with him tomorrow night. At midnight. Neutral territory. Out of town and at the abandoned warehouse over on Bedford Street."

Ransom scowled. "Yeah, I know where it is." His words came out in a low growl, his brow furrowed. It was pretty clear he wasn't happy taking orders, even from his Alpha.

I suppressed a smile; I knew exactly how he felt.

"Good. Then you won't be late," Malone replied.

Ransom gritted his teeth and stared down at the table angrily. I half-expected an outburst from him. A declaration that he wasn't going.

I looked over at Reece, who was pretty tense himself.

Ransom finally pushed away from the table and met Malone's eyes. "I'll be there. On time."

The tension lessened slightly as the men rose from the table.

I stood, but hung back by the table.

Malone and Reece walked to the door, as Ransom silently held it open. Reece left, but Malone turned back and I caught his look, the same intense scrutiny focused on Ransom that had been on me.

"Ransom, tomorrow, midnight," he said firmly. "No running this time. I mean it." Malone held Ransom's gaze for a long moment. His demeanor made it very clear that he needed to obey or he'd catch hell.

Ransom gave him a stoic look. "I'll be there…" He looked at me for a second. "*We'll* be there."

Malone nodded and then left.

27

Hailey

Ransom closed the door. His hand rested on the doorknob for a moment. Finally, he sighed and turned to face me. Even though he was smiling, it didn't come anywhere close to reaching his eyes. It hurt me to see the exhaustion etched on his face. It hurt more knowing that I was the reason all of this was happening.

"You okay?" I asked.

With another sigh, he moved across the room to where I stood and then pulled my head against his chest. "Yeah. I'm okay." He rested his chin on the top of my head. "I guess I'm not very good at taking orders."

"Well, you handled it pretty well, if I do say so myself." I raised my head and our eyes met. "You want to talk about it?"

"No, not now. Maybe later." He let out a weary sigh. "I don't want to think about Jordan, or Travis, or Malone. I want to forget all of that right now. I just want to spend time with you."

I smiled and slid my hand along the fabric of his shirt before resting my cheek against his chest again. The warmth of his body was comforting, the strength of his arms reassuring. I wrapped my arms around his waist and squeezed him hard.

He grunted. "Careful. You're stronger than you look, you know."

I raised my eyebrow. "Sorry. Did I hurt you?"

The corner of his mouth twitched. "My ribs are fine. I'm just messing with you." He pulled me back into his arms and his hands dipped down to cup my buttocks. "You are strong though. For a girl."

I wiggled in his grip and pushed against his chest, laughing. "For a girl? Let me go and I'll show you just how strong I am, Mr. Caveman."

"No way. I've got you where I want you. Almost."

Before I could answer, he picked me up, and tossed me over his shoulder.

I let out a squeal of surprise. "Ransom, you're crazy. What are you doing?"

"Taking you back to bed. Caveman style."

I laughed as he carried me across the living room. I squirmed in his grip, but he reached up and slapped a hand across the seat of my jeans. A delicious heat blossomed between my legs.

"Watch your head." Ransom took me through the bedroom door and then dropped me onto the bed. He climbed in beside me and began tugging at the button on my jeans. "This is what I want," he said, looking down at me. "You and me, just us together."

"Me, too."

His mouth came down on mine. I opened my lips, meeting his kisses hungrily. Soon our clothes were off and my body seemed more alive than ever. I shuddered underneath his touch and arched against his hands as they explored and caressed me. His mouth moved seductively lower until his tongue found the junction between my legs. I moaned as he lavished attention onto my most intimate spots, bringing me over the edge in a matter of seconds. Crying out, I grabbed his hair as the orgasm rippled through me, leaving me trembling and breathless.

Ransom rose and pulled my thighs around his waist. His hips flexed forward and he slid into me, taking his time. It was slow and deliberate. An exquisite torture as he held himself deep inside, barely moving.

I dug my fingers into his hips, urging him on. "Come on, Caveman. I'm not fragile, remember?"

He pulled out and plunged back into me. Then did it again and again. Gasping in pleasure, my hips responded to him and his every move. All the pleasure, the arousal, the animal passion… it all came together, spiraling upward, taking me with it.

This time when I came, it was sudden and violent. Almost overwhelming. As I screamed out my orgasm, I could feel Ransom's movements grow erratic and knew he was right there with me. For a brief moment, I caught a glimpse of the inner beast reflected in his eyes and then felt him shudder in ecstasy. Afterward, Ransom collapsed on top of me and buried his face against my neck.

Relaxing, I closed my eyes and relished the moment of being tangled up with him. The man who'd saved my life. The man I would do anything for. The man I loved, body and soul. There was no other place else I wanted to be, and knew he felt the same.

It was a long time before he raised his head from my shoulder. His face was flushed and his dark hair tangled above his forehead.

I raised my fingers and ran them through the thick strands.

He leaned forward and kissed me softly. "You're the most beautiful thing I've ever seen."

The light in the room had faded and Ransom's face was shadowed. His eyes were a dark blue and heavy-lidded in the dim light.

"I love you, Ransom."

"I love you too, Hailey."

"You know… I never thought I'd say those words, ever, to any man again."

Ransom was silent.

"The last person I said them to was Jordan," I admitted, thinking back to when he'd fooled me into thinking he was a great guy. I'd been so young and naïve.

Just a teenager who'd developed a crush on the Alpha's handsome son. "It seems like another lifetime ago." I drew a deep breath. The memory of the first time I'd met Jordan rose up.

"You don't have to talk about it…"

"I do. I think I do. It's all this crap still floating around in my head. It's like taking out the last of the trash."

Ransom nodded. "Makes sense."

I rested my head on his chest, listening to the steady beat of his heart. The rise and fall of his breathing soothed me.

"How long did you know him?" he asked.

"My dad worked for Travis… you know all that. Did errands… anything he demanded. Everything, I guess, since he was the one Travis sent to…" The words were suddenly lost on my tongue. I felt horrible about my father killing his.

Ransom's hand closed over mine. "Yeah. I know. It was on Travis's orders."

"That didn't make it right."

"No."

I sighed. "When I was young, it seemed like we were always there at Travis's. I practically grew up there. When I got older, Jordan started coming by our house to see my dad. Or, well, that's what I'd thought. At one point, I think it was around the time I turned sixteen, Jordan started bringing me gifts. He'd always been nice to me and, so of course, it really made me feel special. I guess I got lost in the romance and developed a crush on him."

Ransom's grip on my hand tightened briefly. "So, eventually Travis decided you should marry Jordan?"

"Yeah. That was the plan. Apparently it had been the plan all along. I was just too dumb to figure it out."

"It's not your fault, Hailey. You've got to know that. You were manipulated, by Travis and Jordan."

I nodded. "I just wish I hadn't been so gullible."

"He let you see what he wanted you to see."

"He was good at it. Charming, in fact. Whatever he wanted, I would jump at the chance to do. Except... sleep with him." I laughed, a rueful sound in the gathering dark. "It wasn't that I didn't find him attractive. I did. At first. But, I wasn't ready to take that next step, and the more I resisted, the angrier he got. And the more erratic... and mean. That's when the physical abuse started, when I continued to refuse to have sex with him."

Ransom's eyes turned to steel. "Piece of shit."

My eyes filled with tears. Not at the abuse so much, but at how my father hadn't stepped in to help. He'd actually allowed it happen, telling me that I just needed to be nicer and compliant.

The bastard.

Ransom noticed my tears. "Look, babe. You don't have to tell me the rest. He's gone. He can't hurt you anymore."

I sighed. "I feel like I need to get this off my chest. I just... I want you to know everything about me."

He squeezed my hand. "I get it."

I continued. "For so long I thought I was doing something wrong. That it really was my fault. But, every time he tried getting intimate, it repulsed me. I didn't want him touching me with the same hands that caused so much pain."

"You never tried to leave? Before the wedding, I mean?"

"No. I was too scared and didn't know where to go. Not to mention that Jordan kept me on a short leash and scared me into believing that the clan had eyes in every city. He always said that if I tried to run off, I'd get caught and be brutally punished."

Ransom growled in his throat. "The asshole really put you in a bad position... manipulated you. They both did."

The tension in Ransom's body was evident. I could feel the muscles of his arm flexing against my body. I wondered what it would be like when we went to meet

Travis. Would he stay in control, or would Travis push him over the edge? Considering he'd ordered the kill on his father, I knew it wouldn't take much.

"Listen, it's in the past, Ransom." I sat up, turning to face him in the dim light. "I'm fine now. Great, in fact. I don't want to go over all that shit again. There's no point."

Ransom sat up, flicked on the bedside light, and then leaned back against the headboard. So many emotions played across his face: concern, anger. But above all, I saw love. It made my heart swell.

"Ransom, you've changed my life. You've *saved* it. I love you for that." I leaned forward and kissed him gently. When I pulled back, the concern on his face had lessened.

"I love you, too, Hailey." His fingers ran along the side of my face. "You're the most important person in my life right now."

I took his hand, kissing the tips of his fingers. "The feeling is mutual, Ransom."

He pulled me against him in tight embrace before letting me go. "Are you hungry?"

I nodded.

"Me, too. I was thinking maybe Chinese? There's a place up the street that has excellent Lo Mein."

"That sounds wonderful."

He looked at the clock. "It's late… if we don't order soon, the restaurant will be closed. And I'm not sure what I have left to assemble in my kitchen."

"I'm up for whatever it is you want."

His eyes twinkled. "Let's order food first and then we'll discuss round two."

I blushed.

28

Ransom

I stood at the window, looking through the cloudy glass at the overcast sky. We were meeting Travis at midnight; a meeting that could change the course of my life—and Hailey's. With any luck, it would change things for the better. As much as I despised Travis, and wanted justice for my father, I wanted closure more than anything. I wanted to put all of it behind us. I wanted him and his clan to just fade away into the woodwork.

"Are you coming back to bed?" asked Hailey. I could see her reflection in the glass. The sheet was wrapped loosely around her body and her blonde hair spilled across my pillows. For the first time since I'd met her, she looked relaxed. The constant worry on her face, the tension in her body, was gone. She looked content.

"Soon."

I played back the images of everything that had happened last night—and this morning. Hailey was amazing. She was everything I'd ever wanted in a woman, if not more. She was the perfect combination of sensual and arousing, smart and funny.

I turned from the window and stared at her.

She stretched and smiled seductively up at me, her luscious curves playing hide and seek beneath the sheet.

"You truly are a vision."

She laughed and patted the bed. "This vision needs you right now."

Grinning, I moved away from the window as she pulled the sheet aside. I slid in beside her, curling my frame around hers. We fit together so well, her soft curves against my body. Holding her, everything hard in my life seemed softened, smoothed out. Even the hell with Jordan faded a little. I drew a deep breath and inhaled the scent of her hair, her skin, of the two of us together. She rested her hand on my chest, shifting on the pillow so she could look at me. "I could stay here with you forever. I feel so… safe."

I kissed her forehead. "Good. I want you to feel that way."

"I can't remember the last time I just stayed in bed without feeling guilty or anxious." Her face suddenly changed, like a cloud passing over the sun.

I stared at her with concern. "What's wrong?"

"This all might end, depending on what happens tonight."

I shook my head, prepared to say anything to make her feel better, but deep down I knew she was right.

As if reading my mind, Hailey put her hand on my arm. "Don't try to tell me everything's going to be okay. We don't know what Travis's going to say, what he's going to do. He's unpredictable, just like Jordan. He's also a very powerful Alpha."

"A nice combination," I said dryly. "Not to mention, he lost his son. That must have really put him over the edge."

Hailey gave me a rueful smile. "Well, yeah, there is that. But you're his son, too, and there's really no way to predict what he's thinking."

We were quiet for a few moments. Finally, I cleared my throat. Even though I knew what her answer would be, I needed to at least try to talk her out of it. "I really don't want you there tonight, Hailey."

"Do you really think you can keep me from coming along?"

I'd heard the determination in her voice and saw the resolve in her eyes. Malone was right; she was as stubborn as I was.

I nodded, a grudging smile on my lips. "No, I don't think there's any way I could keep you from coming along." I slid one hand up the smooth skin of her thigh. "Except maybe tying you to the bed."

The look she gave made me laugh. The resolve was still there, but her face was flushed pink and there was a seductive smile tugging at the corners of her mouth.

"Maybe after this whole thing with Travis is over, I'll let you tie me up, but for now, I'm coming along. Don't even think about trying to stop me."

The thought of her getting hurt made my chest tighten, but I knew she wasn't going to budge. "Fine, but we do things my way. If I say run, you get the hell out of there. Promise me?"

We stared at each other for a few seconds and then she nodded slowly. "Fine. But, I know him better than you. If I tell *you* to get the hell out of there, you do the same."

I nodded, but only to appease her. When the time came, I'd have to trust my own instincts. Backing away from a fight wasn't something I was planning on. I owed Travis for killing my father and was determined to pay him back.

She sighed and pressed her cheek against my chest. "Thank you."

I kissed the top of her head. "Let's get some sleep."

"Okay."

We closed our eyes, although my mind was racing so much, sleep wasn't even an option. All I could think about was taking down Travis without pissing off my new clan.

29

Hailey

"Hailey. It's time. Wake up," Ransom said grimly.

I snapped awake instantly. The room was gray and somber, a reflection of the weather outside. I could hear the rain tapping against the glass and the distant rumble of thunder. Ransom was sitting on the edge of the bed, his back to the window, fully dressed.

"How long do we have?" I asked, sitting up. Although the room was warm, I felt a chilled to the bone. Enough so that there were goosebumps running along my arms.

"About an hour. We're going to meet Malone and Reece first, to get a good read on the place." He rubbed his hand over my blanket-covered leg. "You want something to eat before we leave?"

"No," I said, my teeth chattering.

"You okay?" he asked, noticing.

"Just a sudden case of nerves." I sighed. "My stomach is in knots."

"Yeah. I know the feeling. At least you got a good nap."

"Have you been awake all this time?"

He nodded. "Yeah. Too keyed up to sleep. Just been pacing the apartment."

"You should have woken me up. At least I could have kept you company. We could have talked or something."

He glanced at me, the shadow of a smile on his face. "No chance. You were out cold. I didn't have the heart. I'll let you get dressed now." He patted my leg, then rose and left the room, closing the door quietly behind him.

I flipped on the bedside light, slid out of bed, and dug around in my duffel until I found a clean pair of jeans and a T-shirt. The last thing I wanted to do was see Travis again, but there was no way I was going to let Ransom do this alone. We were in this together now. All of it.

When I walked into the living room, Ransom stood in front of the window. Hearing me, he turned around. "It's not too late to change your mind, Hailey. You can still stay here."

"Don't think you can get rid of me now, Ransom," I said, walking over to him. I slid my hands around his waist and hugged him.

He rested his chin on the top of my head. "Never."

We held each other for a few seconds more and then he released me. "Let's get this over with."

The ride to the warehouse was surreal, the grimy buildings of the industrial district looming out of the gray fog. I hung on to Ransom as he wove the motorcycle through the deserted streets, finally turning down a narrow, dingy alley between two buildings. We came around the back of the building, and he parked the bike in the shadows of a loading dock. The air smelled of grease and diesel fumes, metal and rust.

"Which building?" I hugged my arms around my chest. The chill that had started in the apartment rose up again, tinged with a perverse sense of anticipation.

"It's actually down the block and over one street. Reece and Malone should already be at the corner. Let's go."

Our steps seemed to echo between the buildings, sounding much too loud.

"It's a good thing we're not sneaking up on anyone," I said dryly.

"Yeah. It's an open meeting, neutral territory and all that bullshit. I'm pretty sure he'll show up with an entourage and a few well-placed and well-hidden bodyguards."

"Great, and it'll just be the four of us?" I asked, struggling to keep up with his long stride. We stopped at the mouth of the alley and Ransom looked each way down the cross street. It was silent, except for the sound of a metallic banging coming from somewhere close by.

"Hell no." His voice was tight, low. "Knowing Malone and Reece, there's a dozen or so clan members hiding out on rooftops and doorways. Malone rarely travels alone, and he never takes any chances."

I relaxed slightly. "Guys from the bike shop?"

Ransom didn't answer.

I peered over his shoulder. The street seemed deserted, just cracked asphalt for blocks in either direction, lit by dim streetlights.

"Come on."

Ransom slipped out of the alley and we started down the street. We passed a few glass-front doors and a trash-filled vacant lot fronted with a chain-link fence. We hurried past the empty lot, and to the corner of the next street.

Slowing down, Ransom whistled a low sound and then repeated it twice.

An answering whistle nearby made me jump. From the shadows of the building, Reece and Malone emerged.

"Ransom. I see you didn't get her to change her mind," Malone said with disapproval.

Reece snorted, a sound between a laugh, and a grunt.

Sick of being talked about like I wasn't there, I opened my mouth to say something when Ransom took my hand. "She can make up her own mind."

"Apparently. We're not here to babysit, though," Malone said.

"I don't need a babysitter," I said tightly.

Malone sighed. "Good. Let's get going before we're late."

The men moved down the street and I followed, nobody saying a word. A short time later, we came to a chain-link fence. Malone stopped and pulled aside the rusted gate. Beyond was a small courtyard, overgrown with weeds, and a broken concrete path, which led to an abandoned building. As we approached, I noticed the door hung on warped hinges and the windows along the front of the building were broken.

Reece pushed aside the door and stepped inside, followed by Malone.

Ransom motioned for me to go next.

Swallowing, I stepped through the door and my boots crunched on broken glass. The odor in the building was pungent, smelling like trash and death.

Ransom followed me in and we stood there silently, looking around.

The large space in front of us stretched back to a bank of high windows. It was filled with rusted out pieces of old machinery and garbage, left by transients and druggies. Everything from old beer cans, to dirty mattresses, and needles.

Since nobody was moving, and everyone looked tense and ready for action, I knew we'd reached the meeting place.

"Malone. About time you showed your face."

Startled, I jumped.

Travis.

His voice had come from somewhere above us. I turned and looked up to find him standing on a second floor tier, smiling down at us derisively.

As usual, he was dressed in an expensive suit, a habit he and his son both shared. His silver hair was combed back from his high forehead, and his blue eyes regarded us with contempt.

Behind him were two guys I recognized, men he'd used as muscle whenever it was necessary. One of them smiled down at me. Duke, or Dude, something like that. He'd always made me uncomfortable. Always leering and making inappropriate comments.

"Travis." Malone smiled back coolly. "Nice of you to join us. Come on down so we can talk face-to-face."

The three men moved to the rusty iron stairway and descended to the main floor. They approached and then arranged themselves across from our group.

Malone stepped forward between Ransom and Reece.

"We're here. Let's get this show on the road. What do you want?" he said.

Travis folded his arms across his chest. "Who's this guy?" He nodded toward Reece.

"You know him. He owns the motorcycle shop," Malone replied.

"Ah, yes. Didn't recognize him out of his element. And you…" He thrust his chin toward Hailey. "You're the whole reason we're in this mess. I have to say, I'm surprised you even showed your face here tonight."

I gave him a dirty look.

Smirking, Travis looked at Ransom, his dark gaze sweeping over him from head-to-toe. "And you're the bastard who killed my son. Lest you take offense, I use the term 'bastard' with the utmost affection since… you are my bastard son."

I could almost see the hair rising on the back of Ransom's neck. His voice was a low, barely controlled growl. "You're obviously very familiar with that term as well, considering your 'son' is the bastard who tried to kill Hailey. And you… you're the bastard who killed my father." Ransom took a step forward, looking ready to take a swing.

I drew a sharp breath, feeling as if all hell was about to break loose. But, before anything could happen, Malone's outstretched arm held Ransom back.

"Both sides lost family." Malone shrugged, his voice calm. "You know as well as I do that shit like this happens in the world we live in. Especially being a shifter. Sorry it was your son, Travis, but he left us with no choice."

Travis kept his eyes on Ransom for a moment longer. "Technically, I had your father killed. But we're splitting hairs." Then he shifted his gaze back to Malone.

Ransom relaxed slightly.

Travis went on. "Let's get to the bottom of what's really important right now. I'm in a very bad position since Jordan is dead. The future of my clan is at stake. I'm not going to be around forever, and there are things that need to be taken care of."

"You need an Alpha to pass the torch to. Now you don't have anyone." Malone's voice was calm, reasonable.

"Actually, you're wrong; I do have someone. I have him. My son." Travis tipped his head in Ransom's direction.

Ransom chuckled coldly. "It'll be a cold day in Hell, Travis, before I call you my 'father'. I don't care about your clan. I have my family. *My* clan. The guys who've had my back all these years."

I glanced at Travis, trying to gauge his mood. I knew nothing pissed him off more than someone disagreeing with him.

Travis shook his head, a cynical smile on his face. "Family. You toss the word around so easily. Do you even know what family really means? I don't think so. It is blood ties, and the responsibility that comes from taking care of your own. You don't have that with these people." Travis pounded his fist against his chest. "But you have that with me. We're blood, Ransom. You can't deny that."

"Travis, nobody is denying the blood ties, but why would you want him to run your clan when he doesn't want to?" Malone's voice had lost its casual tone.

There was a tense moment of silence. I watched, as Travis's eyes flicked dismissively toward Malone before he looked back at Ransom.

"Like it or not, he's in line for it. It's his birthright." He gave Ransom a hard look.

"Birthright?" Ransom's harsh laughter echoed against the walls. "You're crazy. I'm not your clan's next *anything*."

Travis clasped his hands behind him, looking up at the ceiling as if this were just another clan meeting. "Don't you think it's a bit ironic, Ransom? You put yourself in this position. You killed my son, and as my other son, you put yourself in line to be my clan's next Alpha. You did this all on your own."

I looked at Ransom's profile, the narrowed eyes and the clenched jaw. I understood what Travis was saying, knowing how he looked at the world. He was cold and calculating, but it still wasn't easy to swallow. Imagining what was going on in Ransom's mind was impossible.

"I didn't kill Jordan to be your next Alpha. I killed the bastard because he was going to kill Hailey. I was protecting her. Nothing more, nothing less," he snapped back.

"Nothing more..." Travis took a step forward.

Malone and Reece tensed, but stayed where they were.

"I'm going to let you in on a little secret, Ransom. There's always something *more*. And in this case..." Travis took another step forward. The guys behind him both straightened, one flexing his fingers, smirking at me over Travis's shoulder. "I have a bargaining chip. Or you can think of it as an incentive, a way to get you to see things from my perspective… to play this game with me."

"This isn't a game, Travis." Malone moved up behind Ransom.

Travis dismissed Malone with a glance. "You brought it with you, Ransom. Something so precious…" His voice had dropped to a low whisper, a disgusting sound.

"You fucking bastard," growled Ransom. "You leave Hailey out of this."

"I own the bitch," he said with a sneer. "I can do whatever I want."

Having had enough, Ransom rushed forward and took a wild swing at Travis, his fist connecting with his cheek.

Travis let out a bellowing roar of rage. He moved backward, away from Ransom, leaving him to face the two thick-necked bodyguards who stood ready to take him on. There was a flurry of movement, both Reece and Malone running after Ransom, shouting at him, pulling him back.

"Leave him! Get her!" Travis stood, hand to his face, a thick shock of silver hair hanging over his forehead.

I took a step toward Ransom, and that was when strong hands reached around me and pinioned my arms to my sides.

30

Hailey

"Ransom!" I struggled against my captor, someone with arms of steel, and felt my feet being lifted off of the floor.

"Hailey!" He charged toward me with wild eyes. Before he could reach us, the two bodyguards were on him. They had him on the ground faster than I could blink.

I looked over at Reece and Malone, expecting them to react, but they didn't move a muscle.

"Do something!" I cried.

They looked past me and I turned to see more of Travis's goons approaching.

"I can't leave her out of this, Ransom," Travis spat. "She's the center of all of it. Always has been. Hell, she's the reason you killed Jordan." He laughed harshly. "She's the reason you're next in line to be Alpha."

"Jordan is dead because he was a psychotic asshole. If I hadn't killed him, someone else would have eventually," Ransom growled back.

Travis ignored his words. "She was the girl who was going to change everything for me. Give me healthy, strong heirs. Not sick, weak ones like Jordan. Her pure Lycan blood would have neutralized whatever had made Jordan so sick. Keep it from being passed on to their children. I would have had the strongest heirs imaginable. The perfect warriors for my clan."

"There will be no more heirs for your clan," he replied, no longer subdued by the bodyguards. "Not from him. Not from her. None of it matters anymore. You need to let her go." Ransom rose to a crouch.

"Of course it matters," Travis replied.

"You're nothing but a selfish prick. Not to mention a damn coward," he said.

"Coward, huh?" Travis replied calmly. Unlike Jordan, he knew how to control his temper. Better than anyone I'd ever met. He smoothed his hair back, adjusted his tie, and pulled out a snowy white handkerchief. He began dabbing at a cut on his cheek with it. "Or, maybe I'm just playing the game?" He waved his hand, as if he were batting away flies, and then shrugged. "Doesn't matter what you think, anyway. I will get my way on this and there's nothing you can do to stop me."

Having had enough, Reece spoke up. "Travis, you really are a bastard." He took a step toward him, but was cut off by one of the bodyguards, who put a hand to his chest.

"Step back, or you'll regret it." The burly guard pushed and then pushed harder.

"Touch me one more time and you won't live to regret anything ever again." Reece raised his fists.

This time, it was Malone who spoke up. "Reece, don't. There's nothing we can do."

I was amazed at the calmness of Malone's voice. My own heart was hammering so fast, like I'd just run a marathon.

Surely this must be some kind of trick?

Travis looked pleased. "You're a smart man, Malone. You're outnumbered and out-manned. No wonder you're Alpha." The laugh that followed made my skin crawl.

"Ransom. Reece. Let's go." Malone walked over to Ransom and grabbed his hand, pulling him up from the floor.

Ransom looked at me and then back at Malone. "There is no way in hell I'm leaving without her."

"You have to. We're not going to finish this today." Malone muttered.

"Listen to your Alpha, Ransom, like a good boy. Run along now. I'll be in touch." Travis made a shooing motion with his hand, a condescending smile on his face.

Ransom looked like he was going to spring at him, but Malone pulled him away.

"Don't," Malone warned.

Ransom looked at Malone, ready to argue again, when an unspoken message passed between them. His shoulders slumped and he looked at me. "I love you, Hailey. I'll come for you. I promise."

My jaw dropped.

Oh, my God, they are really leaving me?

I watched in horror as Malone propelled Ransom toward the doorway. I couldn't believe they were abandoning me.

"We're not finished, Travis, not by a long shot." Ransom's voice rang angrily through the warehouse. "You and me… it's between you and me now."

The last thing I saw were Ransom's apologetic eyes as Malone shoved him through the doorway. I knew he wasn't thrilled about leaving me, but I still couldn't believe it was happening.

The sound of their footsteps faded and the angry sound of Ransom's voice was the last thing I heard. It shocked me that his clan hadn't put up any kind of fight. From where I was standing, it appeared that they were washing their hands of me. Ransom had been wrong about them accepting me as one of their own. Dead wrong.

Feeling defeated, I hung my head, not wanting anyone to see the tears in my eyes.

"Well, Hailey, you're back with the family. Just like old times," Travis said, sounding proud of himself.

I looked up to find him standing directly in front of me.

He reached out and ran a finger down my cheek. "You really are a beauty. I can see why my son was so obsessed with you. Or should I say, both of them?"

I jerked my head away and spat at him, hitting Travis's expensive tie.

He lurched away, and for a satisfying moment, I watched his composure crack before he pulled himself together again. "Oh, we're so brave now, aren't we, Hailey. I like this new you," he said with a cool smile as he used the handkerchief to daub at the spot I'd left on his tie.

I glared at him. "Why don't you just kill me and get it over with?"

"Kill you? There's no point in causing you any harm. It will only make Ransom angrier. More irrational. You see, I still want him for my Alpha. And you're going to be my bargaining chip."

"He doesn't want it. You heard him."

"Maybe not now, but he will change his mind when he realizes that he can't have you any other way," Travis replied.

"I wouldn't hold my breath. Or better yet, do it and see what that gets you."

Travis tilted his head and smiled. "Feisty little bird. You know, there's no reason we can't be civil to one another until this gets sorted out. I'm going to be the grandfather of your children, you know."

"Keep dreaming."

Shaking his head, Travis motioned toward his men. "Come on, let's get her out of here before they change their minds and come back."

We left the warehouse through a back door. It led to the alley behind the building, where Travis's limo waited.

They bundled me into the backseat and I soon found myself wedged between his two bodyguards, who smelled like sweat and too much aftershave. Travis sat across from us and pulled out his phone.

"Where are you taking me?" I asked, squirming between the guys, not wanting to be touched by either.

"You'll find out soon enough," Travis replied.

Giving up, I sank back into the leather seat, wondering how Ransom would find me. Something told me I was on my own once again. If I was going to escape, I needed to come up with my own plan. There was no way I was going to wait around for Ransom to try and talk his Alpha into helping me. It was obvious that Malone wasn't willing to standup to Travis. Especially just for little old me.

31

Ransom

"So what the hell do we do now?" I muttered, pacing across my apartment and running my hands through my hair. I felt like a royal asshole for letting Hailey down. She'd trusted me and I'd abandoned her. I turned back to the men sitting at my kitchen table, frustrated with everything, including them.

"We wait to hear from Marco. Hopefully he doesn't lose Travis. We'll find where he's taking her and go from there," Malone replied. "We do this together. No going solo on this."

"Wait?" I clenched my jaw. "He could be torturing the hell out of her right now."

"He won't. He needs her healthy and in one piece," Malone replied.

I grunted. "Yeah, that's right. For breeding," I said dryly. "So, what if he rapes her?"

"Don't you get it? He won't lay a hand on her. He's saving her for you," Malone replied. "He's just playing games right now. He's hoping you'll change your mind about everything and come crawling to him."

"How can you be so sure he won't hurt her?" I said.

Malone frowned. "Because he knows how much you care about her. Hell, you'd never make a good poker player. I can tell you that much."

"True," Reece said with a wry grin. "Kid wears his emotions on his sleeve."

Sighing, I dropped into a chair. "I still don't understand why we let her go that easily. I mean, what in the hell happened back there? I thought you said we'd have backup."

With a weary look, Malone pinched the bridge of his nose. "The simple truth is that they brought more muscle than we did. We had guys, but not enough. I didn't want us to get our asses handed to us."

"Yeah," added Reece. "Not to mention that Jack found Dane and Morgan tied up on the roof. They said six or seven guys jumped them alone."

"They okay?" I asked.

Reece nodded and then stood up abruptly. He pushed his chair away from the table. "Fuck, what a mess. I need a drink. What do you have, Ransom?"

I motioned toward the kitchen cupboard. "Whiskey and scotch. Everything's above the fridge. You know where the glasses are…"

"Not sure I'll need one. Might just drink straight from the bottle," he replied.

Malone frowned as Reece banged around in the kitchen. "Hell, pour me some scotch, too."

"Sure." Reece looked at me. "You want some too?"

"May as well," I muttered. "Scotch."

"Sure." Reece set the bottle, along with three glasses, onto the table. He poured us each a decent measure of the scotch and I downed mine in one gulp. The warmth hit me instantly, spreading out from my stomach. I set the glass down, then poured myself another shot.

Reece drank his down and grimaced. "Jeez, Ransom, this is some cheap-ass shit."

"All I can afford with my salary," I jabbed.

Reece grunted.

Malone took a drink and frowned. "We're going to have to teach you to like the good stuff." He pushed his glass away.

"Yeah. I'll work on that." I stared at his empty glass. "So, what? Now we wait?"

"Yeah." Malone's voice was low.

All I could do was shake my head. I knew there was no way that I could take on Travis's crew by myself. I could only hope that Malone was right and Hailey wasn't being harmed. If I found out differently, I'd never be able to forgive myself.

32

Hailey

We drove for a very long time before the limo finally came to a stop. At least two hours. I quickly recognized the ivy-covered wall that guarded the front of Travis's estate.

The limo drove through the gates and up to mansion, stopping in the circular drive in front of the main entrance. The lights were on outside, illuminating the drive and front door.

Someone opened the limo door.

"Careful with her, Duke. She's precious cargo." Travis's voice followed as I was roughly pulled out of the vehicle by Duke.

The other guy slid out after, crowding close behind me. They jostled me up the steps, through the front door, and into the foyer.

I looked around. The house was the same as the last time I'd been there. Angelina, Travis's third wife, had decorated the place and had horrible taste. I'd always thought the place looked less like a home and more like a brothel. Everything was either red or purple, including the wallpaper and carpeting. The woman had been obsessed with the two colors.

I stopped, momentarily blinded by the light from the overhead chandelier that dominated the small space. Duke stood behind me, his hand on the small of my back.

"Come on, sweetheart, move that ass." His hand slid down, and gave me a cruel pinch.

Angry, I spun around to slap him when someone grabbed my wrist and twisted my arm behind me.

It was Travis.

"You'll have to forgive Duke. He's a little excitable," he said with a warning look.

The bones in my wrist screamed in protest, making me suck in my breath to keep from crying out in pain. I didn't want to give them the satisfaction.

"If you promise to be a good girl, I'll let you go. Don't force me to have to tie you up," Travis warned, as I struggled against him.

I froze. If I was tied up, anything and everything could happen. Looking at the smirk on Duke's face, I'd be praying for death if I allowed it to happen.

Sensing my obedience, Travis relaxed. "Good." He released my hand and I rubbed my wrist. "Let's go sit in the living room and have ourselves a little chat. I think we need to go over the house rules. I am willing to let bygones be bygones, if you behave yourself. Understand?"

I didn't believe him, but nodded anyway.

Travis ushered me into his office, all the while talking about starting fresh and making things work. From the way he was talking, it didn't seem as if he was too upset about Jordan being gone.

Listening to him rattle on, I sank down into a wingback chair. He sat down in an oversized leather recliner and pulled out a cigar from his pocket. "You don't mind if I smoke?"

Surprised that he was even asking, I shook my head.

"Good." He cut the end, and lit it. I watched as he sat back and puffed on it before blowing out a cloud of smoke.

"So you've got a champion. Someone who's willing to fight for you. How romantic."

I didn't answer.

He watched me for a moment through the smoke.

"That's the kind of determination will make Ransom an excellent Alpha. He's willing to fight for those he cares about. I respect that more than you know." He drew on the cigar again.

At least he has something worth respecting, I wanted to scream at him. But, I knew it would set him off. "He's not going to be your next Alpha, Travis. He'll come for me, but not for that."

Travis tapped the ash from his cigar into a crystal ashtray. "He'll come. And that's all I care about. The reason is irrelevant."

"Even if it's to kill you?"

"Let him try. Do you think I'm afraid of a young punk like him?"

If he'd seen the way Ransom had taken down Jordan, he wouldn't be talking such big words.

"You'd be a fool not to."

He gave me a dirty look through the blue smoke swirling in front of his cold eyes.

"The only way for this to end well is if you let me go," I said. "You're lying to yourself if you think he's going to walk in here and accept what you have to offer. He'll never do it." Not for him, at least.

"If he doesn't accept, both of you will die."

"You're as crazy as your son," I replied, unable to help myself.

Glaring at me, he stood up. "Your father failed in the manners department. Talking to your Alpha like that."

"My father failed in a lot of things," I countered.

"I think it's time we shut you up." He set his cigar down and pulled his cell phone out.

My heart began to pound. "What are you going to do?"

He didn't reply but began texting someone.

I stood up.

"Sit your ass down," he ordered.

Before I could say anything, the door opened and Duke walked in, carrying duct tape and rope.

"Tie her up. She's getting on my nerves," Travis said, grabbing his cigar from the ashtray.

Duke smirked. "My pleasure."

33

Ransom

"She's at Travis's house. The one on Mont Blanc Boulevard, in Farmington," Malone said after hanging up his phone. "From what it looks like, he only has a couple of bodyguards with him."

That was all I needed.

I was already at the door before Reece could speak.

"Slow down, cowboy. Where do you think you're going?" he asked.

"To get her," I said firmly. They didn't look like they were in much of a hurry and I couldn't wait around any longer. Every second that had ticked by, the sense of doom had grown stronger. Maybe I couldn't take down all of Travis's men, but I'd find another way. I had to.

"Do you even know where the hell you're going, Ransom?" Malone asked.

I shrugged. "I know where Farmington is. I'll figure out where Mont Blanc Boulevard is and then go from there." I calculated it to be about a two-hour drive.

"And be totally overwhelmed. And most likely get your ass killed," Reece said angrily.

"As big and fucked up as this mess is, it's my mess. It's between me and Travis. He's dragged Hailey into this, and she's my… she's the most important thing in my life. I need to do this, whatever it is. However it works out."

"Your heroics are going to get you killed," he replied. "You can't go storming over there by yourself."

Looking at Reece, I knew I couldn't drag him along into this. I didn't want to lose another person in my life I cared about, and he wasn't a spring chicken. I couldn't put him in this kind of danger. "You've always been there for me, always had my back. But now, I've got to do this alone."

"You can't…" he protested.

"Yes, I can."

Malone spoke up. "He's right. He can and should."

Startled, we both looked at him.

"This really is between the two of them," Malone added.

Reece scowled. "You can't let him do this on his own. It's pretty much sending him to his death."

"Reece, he's not just some kid off the street. You know that and so do I. Besides, Ransom here has a motive to succeed that neither of us have." He looked at me.

"What's that?" Reece's voice held resignation.

I knew what he was getting at. And he was right. I looked over at my old friend and mentor, the man who'd always taken me back time after time. Reece looked exhausted, his face drawn, dark circles beneath his eyes.

"The kid is head-over-heels in love. We're just old guys in a pissing contest with Travis." Malone jerked his thumb toward me. "His heart is involved and he'll put everything he has into getting her back."

"But, he'll be alone," Reece protested.

"We go out there as a group, someone will catch our scent. He goes in by himself, he has a better shot of sneaking in and getting her out of there," Malone said. "Besides, Travis isn't surrounded by his entourage, like usual."

"Why do you think that is?" Reece asked.

"Travis is an arrogant son-of-a-bitch who thinks he can take care of himself," I answered for him.

"Yes, and he can," Malone said. "He wouldn't be Alpha if he needed someone to do his fighting."

I nodded.

Reece's shoulders slumped. "I guess there's no talking you out of it then?"

"No way," I replied.

Sighing, he stood up and put his hand on my shoulder. "Fine, you go alone, Ransom, but you damn well better come back," he said, getting a little choked up.

His concern for me warmed my heart. "I will."

He pulled me into a rough hug, held me briefly, and then released me. He then walked over to the window and stared outside, his back to us.

"Ransom…" Malone stood up. "You're either the bravest motherfucker I've ever met, or the most foolish." He held out his hand.

I shook it. I didn't feel brave, so that left a fool. I didn't care, though. Hailey needed me and I wasn't about to let her down again. She'd had enough bullshit in her life. I was determined to do everything in my power to bring her back. Even if it meant killing Travis.

34

Ransom

Ten minutes later, I was on my bike and heading out of town, through the back roads. I'd gotten rough directions from Malone, but knew in my heart I'd locate Hailey without it. As long as I found Mont Blanc Boulevard and the house Malone described. Apparently, it was the biggest and ugliest in the neighborhood.

The ride seemed to take forever, mostly because I couldn't stop worrying about her. Even if Travis wasn't harming her physically, she had to be going through a lot of mental abuse. I was still kicking myself for giving up so easily and walking out of the warehouse. Especially after promising her that I'd never let anything bad happen to her. Now, here she was in the enemy's house, alone and feeling abandoned. I should have fought tooth-and-nail to get her away from Travis and his posse.

When I finally arrived in Farmington, I tracked down Mont Blanc Boulevard, which was home to a multitude of mansions, set back from the street. Because it was still a few hours from dawn, the neighborhood was quiet and sparse.

I almost laughed out loud when I found Travis's. It was large, by far *the* largest, and certainly the ugliest, as Malone had mentioned. The outside looked like it had been designed for someone lacking attention. Tudor beams competed with Italianate columns while Rococo flourishes adorned almost every surface.

Awful.

The mansion itself stood on a hill, behind an ivy-covered wall. Of course he had to be up high, looking down on everyone else.

I drove slowly past and parked two streets over before returning on foot. I noticed the back of the property overlooked the edge of an industrial park and looked nothing like the front. There wasn't even an ivy-covered wall, just a chain-link fence. Unlike the front, it was finished with plain red brick and a series of windows on the second floor. It definitely was a jarring and odd contrast to the front of the home. It almost looked as if Travis had spent more money on the visible parts of the house, and had said 'screw it' to the back.

After jumping over the fence, I circled around the house, my senses on alert. Fortunately, there didn't appear to be anyone outside guarding the place. Or, cameras for that matter. I thought it was odd, especially with how many enemies Travis and Jordan must have had.

Creeping back around, I briefly caught Hailey's scent and was relieved that she'd not blocked it. It was heavy with fear and it tore at my heart and made my blood boil. Then it was lost in the conflicting scents of the neighborhood, of the other Lycan in the house, and some of the pets in the neighborhood. But it wasn't important. I'd found Hailey. That was all that mattered.

Keeping low to the ground, I crept closer and that was when the back door opened. Swearing under my breath, I sprinted behind a tree just as one of the guys from the warehouse stepped outside. There was a brief flicker of a match and then the sharp smell of cigarette smoke. The guy leaned against the door and idly blew smoke toward the sky. After a few more drags, he turned and stubbed his cigarette out against the side of the building.

With his back turned, I raced over and put my arm around his mouth. Before he could sound off an alarm, I pressed my hand against his carotid artery. He only struggled for a moment before his body went limp. Relaxing, I dragged him back into the shadows before running back to the door and slipping inside. Moving slowly, I listened intently to the sounds of the house. It wasn't long before I heard Travis's voice, near the front.

Alone, in a small, dark hallway, I stopped and sniffed the air. The house smelled overwhelmingly of perfume, wood cleaner, and deodorizer. I drew a deeper breath and closed my eyes to concentrate. Beneath the cloying scents of artificial flowers and citrus, I also smelled sickness and decay.

I opened my eyes up and snuck down a different hallway, where there were several doorways. I moved forward cautiously, looking through each of them. One opened into a closet and another appeared to lead to a basement. The next doorway led to a massive gourmet kitchen.

As I crept past, the voice down the hallway grew louder. I recognized it as Travis's and he was droning on and on about staying loyal to the clan and how blood was thicker than water.

Moving forward, I stopped just before the hallway opened up to the foyer. A dim, formal-looking living room was to the left. To the right was the room I wanted.

I stopped at the edge of the archway, every sense on alert. Hailey was definitely there. I could hear her breathing and her scent was strong. I didn't pick up anything else, besides Travis's cologne, and knew they were alone in the room.

"Ransom. Welcome. Stop skulking in the hall. Please, come in," Travis called out.

Sighing, I put my hand on the doorknob and for a moment, hesitated. My impulse was to charge in with guns blazing and tear into the asshole. Instead, I squared my shoulders and stepped into a large office.

I saw Hailey first. She was seated in a paisley wingback chair and her bright eyes were filled with relief as we stared at each other. Her hands were tied behind her and there was duct tape over her mouth.

Travis smiled. "We've been expecting you, Ransom. I've been telling Hailey how life is going to be from now on, once you realize it's futile to fight me."

I glared at him. "I'll kill you before I agree to anything you have to say, Travis."

Travis stood up. "You're so predictable, Ransom. So narrow-minded." He took a step forward. "Can't you, just for one moment, imagine what it would be like to be the Alpha of this clan? You'd have everything you'd ever wanted. You'd be able to give Hailey everything she's ever wanted."

I took in the man standing across from me.

Something was off.

In fact, there was something wrong with the entire place. The way it smelled, and with Travis himself. He was still dressed in the same suit, sans tie, the starched white shirt unbuttoned at the throat. His hair was carefully arranged. Everything was perfect. Except for the cut on his cheek. It hadn't yet healed. It should have by now.

Travis took another step toward me "You'd have power, Ransom. And power is sexy." Travis's voice had dropped to that confidential tone he'd used at the warehouse. It grated on my nerves.

I grunted. "You're still barking up the wrong tree, Travis. I'm not interested in power or being sexy. That's your show, not mine."

Travis laughed, an irritating sound that made me grit my teeth. Travis moved slowly behind Hailey's chair. He set his hand lightly on her shoulders, making her flinch.

Anger boiled up in me. I didn't like him touching her. "If you're done listening to the sound of your own voice, how about you let Hailey go? This is between you and me. Stop hiding behind a girl."

"I'm not hiding behind anyone." Travis set his other hand on Hailey's shoulder. "This is your fate, Ransom.

You can't run away from this, like you've run away from everything else in your life."

There was a whimper from Hailey.

My eyes moved from her to Travis's hands. He was digging his fingers into her shoulders so hard his knuckles were turning white.

Knowing he was hurting her threw out the last bit of restraint I possessed. With a fierce growl, I lunged at Travis, hitting him in the shoulder, spinning him away from Hailey. Her chair tipped over, and she toppled away from him, hitting the floor with a thud.

Distracted by Hailey's groan of pain, I wasn't ready for Travis's quick response. He slammed his fist into the side of my head. The blow threw me off balance and my head began to ring. I staggered, catching sight of Hailey on the floor, her eyes wide with fear. Her vulnerability made me want to tear Travis's throat out. He was an Alpha, though. Still the strongest of his clan. There'd be only one way to beat him.

Closing my eyes, I threw my head back, my scream echoing against the walls as I forced the shift through me. Changing this quickly hurt like hell.

When I dropped back down to the floor, the pain was gone and adrenaline surged through me. I was ready to fight.

Travis, still standing over Hailey, looked less confident as he stared at me. It was gratifying to see, but short-lived. His lips slanted into a smirk as he began shifting, apparently not as intimidated as I'd hoped. I watched with a strange feeling of helplessness as Travis dropped to the floor, now a massive gray Lycan, with ebony eyes.

We stood facing each other and I had no illusions that the man—or wolf—would fight fair. And… I wasn't going to, either. Not after everything that had happened.

I dove forward, knocking him into the wall. Oddly, for his size, Travis felt light, hollow… insubstantial. I sank my teeth into his shoulder. A familiar foul taste filled my mouth and it hit me; Travis was diseased, just like Jordan had been. He reeked of decay and rot. His blood and hide tasted of death. For a brief instant I wondered if it was also my destiny.

Before I could finish the thought, Travis twisted out of my grip. He snapped at me, biting me in the neck, drawing blood.

Yelping, I twisted out of his grip.

He scrambled away, claws scratching on the hardwood floor as he retreated. I hadn't injured him that badly, but he already seemed dazed, shaking his head violently while whimpering and whining.

I leapt at him again, driving him to the floor until I was able to sink my teeth into his shoulder. He knocked me away tried biting me back, but only managed to snap mouthfuls of air.

I watched and waited, dodging Travis's snapping fangs until I was able to bite him again. Just as before, the taste was horrific but I held on, my jaws tearing deeper into his pelt. A wave of blood washed over my jaws, hot and coppery mixed with a sickening taste that made me want to gag. But, I held on as he thrashed beneath me. Images flashed through my mind—my father being murdered. Jordan dragging Hailey from the cabin and later standing over her in the woods with that evil grin. Just remembering drove me over the edge. Growling, I tore at Travis, taking my rage out on him.

He emitted a sickening, gargled noise and soon his struggles grew weaker. But I was too caught up in my fury and kept attacking long past the point where Travis had stopped struggling. It wasn't until I heard a whimper behind me that I let go and backed away from the still form, half-expecting him to leap to his feet.

Pulling myself together, I turned around to see Hailey struggling with her ropes, her eyes locked on mine. I went over and tugged at them with my canines, undoing the knot. When it was loose, she shook off the ties, then pulled the tape from her mouth.

"Ransom. My God." She sat up, staring at Travis's body. "You actually killed him. Just… just like that, too. I can't believe it."

I looked at his still form, still not quite believing it myself. I'd expected more of a fight. Especially for an Alpha. Of course, he was older and whatever disease that had been running through him had surely made him weak. What that meant for me, I still wasn't sure.

She looked at the doorway. "We need to get out of here, Ransom. Someone's bound to come back. Let's go."

35

Hailey

We made it out of the office and down the hallway. That was when we ran into Duke.

"Going somewhere?" he asked, pointing a gun in our direction.

"Stay out of this," Ransom said. He moved between us. "Before you get hurt."

Duke laughed. "I'm the one holding the gun, pal."

"It's over," I said. "Travis is dead."

His eyes widened in surprise. "I don't believe you. That would mean…" his eyes met Ransom's, "you're the new Alpha then, right?"

"I don't want the job," Ransom said firmly. "Hell, you can have it for all I care."

"It doesn't work that way," Duke said, although I could tell from his voice that he was intrigued with the idea.

"That's not my problem," Ransom replied and sniffed the air. "By the way, this house smells like death. Not just Travis's. Someone should check that out."

"Where is Travis?" Duke asked.

"In his office," Ransom replied.

The two men stared at each other and then Duke lowered his eyes. He put his gun back into his jacket and without another word, headed back to where we'd left Travis.

"Well, that went much easier than I thought," Ransom said, when we were outside.

"Yeah. I don't think Duke knew what to do. On one hand, you're the enemy. On the other, you're Travis's son. At least he was smart enough to walk away."

Ransom nodded.

"Where are Malone and Reece?" I asked.

"They stayed behind."

"You snuck out here to rescue me?"

"No, they knew I was going."

"Were they angry?"

"Just worried more than anything."

"So worried that they followed you out here," I said dryly.

"This was between me and Travis. I had to face him alone."

I let out a sigh. Thankfully, things had ended up the way they did. It could have went an entirely different way, especially if more of Travis's clan members had been around.

Ransom grabbed my hand. "It's over. We're finally free of them."

I nodded.

It took us almost three hours to return to Briar Lake, mainly because we stopped along the way for a quick bite to eat. When we finally made it back to his apartment, I crawled in bed, exhausted. A short time later, he walked out of the bathroom, wearing a towel.

"How do you feel? Do you need anything?" He sat down on the edge of the bed.

"I'm good. Really. You can stop asking." Ever since we'd returned from Travis's, he'd been fretting over me unnecessarily. In fact, he'd been treating me like a fragile china cup, and it was beginning to drive me crazy.

He gave me a concerned look. "You sure?"

"Yes."

"I just can't stop thinking about how we left you at the warehouse. I was so pissed off. I—" His words were cut off by a knock on the door. He groaned. "Dammit, I'm really not in the mood to talk to anyone. And by anyone, I mean Reece or Malone."

The knocking resumed, louder and more insistent. The noise Ransom made this time was clearly a growl.

"But you know they're not going away. They obviously know we're here, too." I pulled my hand gently away from his. "You need to talk to them. There's a whole hell of a lot that's happened in the last few hours."

"Yeah. I know." He rose, dropping the towel to the floor, reaching for his jeans. For a fleeting instant, watching him standing naked at the foot of the bed, I shared Ransom's wish that everyone would just leave us alone. But he pulled on his jeans and left the room.

I listened to him open the door and heard muted voices. I recognized Malone's and Reece's, but there were other voices too. Whoever they were, they sounded excited.

I slid off the bed, dressed quickly, and then headed into the living room.

Reece and Malone were there, along with two other men I'd never seen. The tension in the room was almost visible, most of it radiating from Ransom. He glanced at me, his look unreadable, then turned back to Malone.

"We might as well all sit down and get this over with. It's obvious you have something you want to tell me that couldn't wait," Ransom said.

Malone looked at me and then back to Ransom. "Yeah, well, obviously a lot of shit has come up that needs to be dealt with."

"Yeah, thanks for filling us in on what's been happening," Reece added sarcastically.

"Sorry. I was going to. We haven't been home very long," he replied, walking over to the dining table. He pulled out a chair for me and then nodded toward the other two. "May as well make yourself at home."

Reece and Malone sat down while the two strangers stood uneasily with their arms folded. They were big and burly, taking up a whole lot of space in the tiny apartment. Ransom eyed them warily. "Who's the muscle? You traveling with bodyguards now, Malone?"

Malone flicked his eyes at the guys, then frowned at Ransom. "They're not muscle. Or at least, they're not mine. They're from Travis's clan."

Ransom looked angry. "What the hell are they doing here? You invited the enemy into my apartment? That takes some balls, Malone. Even for you."

"Calm down, Ransom. They're not the enemy. They're here about what happened to Travis. And about what happens next. What you plan to do," he replied.

"What *I* plan to do? I'm not planning to do anything except live my life in peace." Ransom crossed his arms, frowning at Malone.

Reece leaned forward, eyeing Ransom intently. "Listen, son, you killed Travis. You killed one of the most powerful Alphas around. You knew going in that there would be consequences. And now it's time to face them."

As strong and as powerful as Travis had once been, even I'd noticed that Ransom had taken him down easily. Almost *too* easily. It almost made me wonder if somehow... Travis had wanted it that way.

"I'm not going to be the Alpha of Travis's clan even if he was my biological father. The only reason I walked into that house willingly was to get Hailey. Killing him... well," he shrugged. "Travis hurt Hailey and attacked me. What else was I supposed to do?"

"There's something you didn't know," Malone went on, leaning back in his chair. "You're not the only one who wanted Travis out of the picture."

Ransom sat forward, eyes locked on Malone. "What are you talking about?"

Malone looked back at the strangers. "This is Levi and Crow. They're part of Travis's clan… *your* clan, Hailey." He threw me a pointed look.

I had no idea who these men were, and it irritated me that Malone expected me to recognize them.

"Tell him what you told us," Malone said to the strangers.

Levi started talking. "It's been… difficult… with Travis as Alpha. He'd become erratic and more violent since…" Levi looked at me.

"Since you left Jordan at the altar." Crow spoke over Levi's shoulder. His voice was sharp and he looked me directly in the eye as he said the words. "Sorry, but that's the truth."

"Travis's violent behavior can only be blamed on himself," Ransom said sternly. "She has nothing to be sorry about."

I relaxed.

"So, Travis changed just because of *that*?" Malone asked, surprised.

Crow and Levi nodded.

"Yeah. Not to mention that Jordan went insane, or more insane. I guess they both went off the deep end at the same time," Crow said.

"We respected Travis as our Alpha. He could be an asshole at times, but… he'd been more or less fair. Afterward…" Levi shrugged. "Everyone got hit by his change of attitude. From his staff, his bodyguards, all the way down through the ranks. There's even a rumor that Travis killed his wife."

"Yeah, nobody has seen her. We think she's either dead, or locked away in some room in the house," Crow added.

Ransom turned to me, his eyes dark. We'd both smelled something horrible in the house. I shuddered, suddenly overcome with an image of myself as Jordan's wife. In a rage, I could almost see him leaving me for dead or stuffed in a closet somewhere in the house.

"You think he murdered her? You can't blame Hailey for that if he did," Reece said.

"We're not saying it's her fault. Whatever was wrong with them, with Jordan and Travis, it started long before that. But, things went downhill pretty quickly from there."

"And how is this any of my problem?" Ransom asked, irritated.

Levi shrugged. "We need an Alpha. You not only killed ours, but Jordan as well."

"We're not complaining about it, by any means," Crow added in quickly. "In fact, we're impressed. We think you'd make a good leader. Hell, you're part of the family, anyway, whether you like it or not."

Ransom's eyes narrowed. "How many times do I have to say I don't want to be Alpha? Are you all deaf? And you're not my family. I'm done with all of you." He pushed himself away from the table, knocking over his chair.

Levi and Crow took a step back while Reece reached for Ransom's arm, but Ransom shook him off. Everyone seemed to be in motion, talking at once, except Malone.

"Ransom." Malone's commanding voice cut through the noise, and confusion. "Sit down."

I waited more of an outburst, but Ransom stood there silently with his fists clenched at his sides.

We hadn't had a lot of sleep and I knew the stress was getting to him. That, and the fact that he didn't want anything more to do with Travis or Jordan. But, I also knew our customs and you couldn't always just walk away from it. Even if you wanted to.

I reached out to him, my fingers brushing against his clenched fist. He flinched but his hand relaxed, not quite unclenching, but just enough to let me slip my fingers inside his.

"You've set this in motion and I get where you're coming from. None of this was your idea and you're not happy with any of it." Malone sat forward, resting his hands flat on the table. "You've been thrust in situations all your life. Your father's murder. Getting passed around as a kid. Trying to fit in with strangers. I know it's been rough and not your fault. But," he stood up, "you need to stop running, Ransom. Every time something gets rough, you bolt. It's time to face the situation."

Malone held Ransom's gaze.

Levi and Crow exchanged nervous glances while Reece shifted in his chair.

Ransom and Malone stared at each other for a long time and I held my breath, waiting for something to break. For someone to give in. In the end, it was Ransom who made the first move. He blew out a small breath, some of the tension draining from his body. He dropped his eyes to the table.

Malone sighed. "You'll do what's right, Ransom. I know you will. Just, give it some thought." Without another word, he turned toward the door and headed out with Levi and Crow following.

Reece rose slowly, a weary expression on his face. He walked around the table and set his hand on Ransom's shoulder. "You know if I could, I'd change all this. But Malone is right. You…" Reece glanced down at me, his face softening for a moment. "Both of you need to think about what comes next. Malone's right, you can't run away from this. It's too big. Promise me you won't run this time."

"Yeah. It's big and it's all mine," he replied sardonically.

"You'd make a good leader," Reece said, ignoring the sarcasm. "A fair one."

"How do you know? I don't feel like I could lead anyone," Ransom said. "Let alone be the Alpha of a clan."

"You're brave. Stupidly so, sometimes," Reece joked. "But, you have courage and determination. That's a good start."

Ransom still didn't look convinced.

"Listen to me," Reece said. "The world is a better place without Travis and Jordan. That's because you did something about it. I don't care about the 'why' you did it. Yeah, we all know it had nothing to do with power. But, the truth remains that you took out an Alpha and the crazy bastard who would have replaced him. Now, their clan wants you to lead. They respect you. You should feel pretty good about that."

Ransom shrugged.

Reece went on. "You know you'll always have a place in our clan, but let's face the facts… you were destined to run your own. It's in your blood, whether you like it or not."

From Ransom's expression, I could tell that he didn't.

Reece sighed. "Well, I'll get out of your hair. Seems you have a lot of thinking to do. Just… don't let your feelings for Travis and Jordan get in the way. You could be doing a dishonor to a clan who could use a good, strong leader."

"I'm younger than most of them," Ransom said. "Inexperienced. Why would they want me, aside from the fact that I overpowered and killed their Alpha?"

"Respect. They didn't respect Travis. Not anymore, at least. They obviously respect you," he replied. "Not to mention, Malone's put in a good word for you, too. I may have as well."

"Maybe you could put in a good word for my boss at work? I could use a raise," he joked.

Reece chuckled. "Listen, kid, if you're Alpha of that clan, you can be your own boss. Give yourself a raise."

Ransom didn't reply.

"Just, give this some real thought. Okay?" Reece said.

Ransom nodded.

Reece winked at me and then turned and left the apartment.

Ransom sighed. "I really dragged you into some kind of hell here, didn't I?"

"I'm the one who dragged you into this, not the other way around. You could have walked away at the beginning, and not helped me get away from Jordan."

The room suddenly seemed very bright, way too bright, especially for this conversation. I wanted to be in the dark, in Ransom's bed, and in his arms.

I stood up and held my hand out.

He raised his eyebrow, reached out, and took my hand.

"You have something to say about all of this?"

"Maybe. I want to talk about this lying down. Preferably naked."

That got a laugh from Ransom.

He followed me into the bedroom.

I drew the blinds and then walked over to him. I reached out and tugged the zipper down on his jeans.

"You're pretty determined to get your way, aren't you?" Despite his words, he didn't resist my efforts and grabbed the edge of my T-shirt.

I stopped what I was doing long enough to let him pull the shirt over my head. He dropped it to the floor. His jeans followed, and then mine. I wrapped my arms around him and rested my cheek on his chest. The touch of his hands on my back, as he folded me into his arms, was exactly what I'd wanted.

I looked up at him, his face in the shadows, but his eyes bright. "I love you."

"I love you, too."

I stood on my tiptoes and kissed him softly before drawing him to the bed.

"You know we're going to have to pick sides one of these days." His voice was low in the dark.

"Pick sides? Between Malone and Travis's clan?" I frowned, pulling the blankets up.

"No. I mean 'sides of the bed'. We never talked about it, and if you have a preference…"

I snorted. "I don't have a preference. And you're trying to avoid the elephant in the room, Ransom."

He pulled me against him. "Yeah. I suppose I am. But, I'm more interested in the girl in my bed." His lips brushed against my neck while one hand caressed my hip.

"Ransom, I really do think we need to talk about—"

His lips cut off my words, his kiss all-consuming. I kissed him back as one hand slid up my side to my breast. Heat blossomed deep inside, sweet and intense. For a moment I gave in, letting my body take control.

"Ransom…" I broke the kiss, gently pushing him away. "You're avoiding it again."

He sighed. "The elephant… yeah. Okay."

We rearranged ourselves in the bed and I rested my head on his shoulder.

"So… you think I should do it, become Alpha?" he asked, staring up at the ceiling.

I'd put a lot of thought into it myself, and knew that Reece had been right. He'd make a good one. Besides, after what Travis had done to his father, he deserved a better life. Being an Alpha, and the only living relative of Travis's, he'd inherit everything. Even if he didn't want the money, he could do something useful with it.

"I think you should seriously think about it."

"You'd actually want me to be the Alpha of the clan that almost got you killed?" he asked, shocked.

"It wasn't the clan that almost got me killed. It was Jordan… and Travis. And they're gone now."

He was silent for several seconds. "You really think I have what it takes to take on that kind of responsibility?" The doubt in his voice almost broke my heart.

"You're smart, and brave, and fearless. Besides, you've taken pretty good care of me. I think taking care of a clan would probably be easier."

His laugh was a low rumble against my cheek. "Yeah, you're a handful, all right. Not sure how I manage." He leaned over, kissing my forehead. "And I love you. That makes a little bit of difference."

"You don't have to do this alone, you know. You've got Malone, Reece… me. It sounds like you also have a clan who would be happy to have you as their Alpha."

Ransom made a non-committal noise.

"At least two of them want you," I reminded him. "As for Duke, he's a creep but… he'll accept you."

Ransom went silent for a long time. I listened to his breathing and his heartbeat under his chest. After a long time, he drew a deep breath, held it for a second, and then blew it out.

"I suppose it is the right thing to do."

I nodded.

"I mean, I did kill the Alpha."

"And it's tradition that you take his place."

"Yeah." The doubt was gone from his voice. "I guess I'd better keep 'tradition' going."

"Well, yeah."

"Okay. I'll talk to Malone and schedule a meeting with the clan. But not until tomorrow. I want this day to be ours."

I propped myself up on one elbow, watching his face in the soft light. "It's going to be okay, you know?" I rested one hand on his chest, right over his heart. "It's both of us now. We're in this together."

"Yeah, I know." He took my hand, raised it to his lips and brushed a kiss across my knuckles. "I'll be honest though, if you weren't here, I'd just say fuck it and take off."

"If I wasn't here… none of this would be happening. This mess is all because of me," I replied, feeling guilty again.

"It's not your fault. It's just the way things got played." He kissed the top of my head. "Anyway, it's all been worth it. You're worth it, Hailey. Without you, I'd just be some lonely soul, working at Reece's, leaving when things got tough, and crawling back when I got tired of living on the road."

I smiled.

He blew out a long breath. "I'm willing to give it a try. But if it gets between us… at all, in any way… I'm done. They can find someone else."

"Okay."

"Now, enough about all of this." He leaned down and started kissing me.

I closed my eyes, his lips firm against mine, his tongue flicking against my mouth. I parted my lips, meeting his kisses fully.

The kiss deepened and became more passionate. There was a need I felt, echoed in Ransom's kiss. Something deep and primal, an overwhelming desire to come together, to take as well as give. I wanted him, his strength, his warmth, his protection. I was pretty sure Ransom wanted the same, and I'd do anything in my power to give it to him. Body and soul.

It wasn't long before I was moaning and responding to Ransom's hands and mouth. I begged for him to take me and he reached down between my legs, finding my wetness. Growling, he positioned himself between my thighs and with a savage thrust, did just that.

Gasping in delight, I met his hips with mine, loving the feel of him inside of me, moving in and out.

Everything seemed to spiral upward as our bodies moved in a dance that felt both new and familiar. Faster and faster he drove into me, driving me wild with desire as he brought me closer to orgasm.

With a final thrust he lifted his head with his breath rasping from his throat. Seeing the way his voice twisted in ecstasy drove me over the edge. I cried out, arching against him, meeting his solid weight as he pinned me to the bed.

He filled me with such powerful heat, I thought I would melt into the bed.

I went limp, enjoying the waves of pleasure as they crashed through me.

Ransom shuddered against my body, his open mouth pressed against my shoulder, savoring the moment as well.

In the soft light, we held each other for a long time, each reluctant to let go of the other. Ransom finally raised his head and I caught the glint of his eyes.

"We're getting pretty good at this." His voice was soft, slightly rough around the edges, and still more than a little breathless.

I smiled, my fingers tracing the contours of his. "Yeah. Well, practice makes perfect, you know."

"I agree." He shifted, rolling onto his side next to me. For a moment I felt weightless before his arm slid across my stomach, pulling me back to earth.

We lay there quietly for a few minutes and then I squeezed his forearm. "I love you, Ransom. I want you to know that no matter how this turns out, it's not going to change how I feel about you."

He smiled. "Thanks for that. I have no idea in hell how this is even going to work. Or, if the rest of the clan will even accept me. But, having you in my corner is all that matters."

"I will *always* be in your corner."

He kissed my knuckles. "If you're going to be there, we should make it official then."

My eyes widened. "What do you mean?"

"Marry me."

Tears sprang to my eyes. It was totally unexpected and caught me off guard. "What?"

"Be my wife. The mother of my children. The woman I grow old with. My… mate."

"Are you sure?" I asked, my heart filling with so much love for him that my chest suddenly felt ten sizes too small.

"I've never been *more* sure of anything in my life, Hailey. I don't want a future without you and I want everyone to know that we come as a package deal. Besides, loving you has shown me that I can look my problems in the face without running. I'm not afraid of anything anymore. Just… losing you."

"That's nothing you'll ever have to worry about," I whispered, brushing the tears from my cheek.

He smiled. "So, you'll have me?"

"Yes. Of course."

Ransom looked relieved.

"There is one condition, though."

His eyebrow arched.

"With our track records, we should probably walk down the aisle chained to each other. With my luck, you'll get the last minute jitters and take off," I teased.

"Not a chance. Besides, you're the one afraid of altars, not me."

"As long as you're standing at it, never."

He laughed. "Maybe we should just elope on a small island. Not tell anyone."

"Somehow, I think Reece would be truly hurt. He loves you, you know."

Ransom smiled. "I love him, too. He'll be my best man, no matter where we get hitched."

"Crap, who'll be my maid of honor?" I said and smiled. "Malone? I wonder how he'd feel in a dress."

Ransom threw his head back and laughed.

"Maybe we could talk him into a kilt?" I added.

"That would be priceless. Maybe I should make that a condition of accepting the Alpha position?"

We looked at each other and both of us burst out laughing.

Ransom's phone began to ring. He picked it up and looked at me. "It's Malone."

"You'd better answer it."

He nodded and brought the phone to his ear. "Hey, what's up?"

Malone spoke from his end and when he was finished, Ransom looked at me with a grim expression. "At least they found out what happened to her," he replied.

"What's going on?" I whispered.

"They found Travis's wife's body in the basement. Under some floor boards," he explained.

I shuddered. That explained the smell.

The two spoke for a few more seconds and then hung up.

"Did he ask about you being Alpha again?"

"No, but I'll give him my answer this week. We're supposed to get together for breakfast."

"And you're not going to change your mind?"

"No. For once in my life, I feel like everything is finally starting to fall into place." He pulled me into his arms and kissed the top of my head.

I closed my eyes and sighed happily. "Me, too."

Epilogue

Hailey
One Year Later

3:48 A.M.

"Ransom. Ransom, wake up," I said, shaking his arm. We were living in Travis's old house, which we'd gutted and remodeled to make our own. He was now the Alpha of Travis's clan, although some of the members had moved on, like Duke. Thankfully, those who'd stayed treated Ransom with respect. They were also trustworthy, dependable, and dedicated. Not to mention that they were all relieved to finally have a level-headed leader. Things were going well for us and everything seemed to be falling into place.

He opened his eyes. "What is it?"

I rubbed my pregnant belly. "It's time."

Suddenly wide awake, Ransom sat up quickly. "You're sure?"

Another contraction hit me. I squeezed his forearm as the pain rippled through me. "Yes. We need to call Dr. Frazer," I said through clenched teeth.

"Breathe, babe. Remember to breathe like they told you at that Lamaze class."

"I have been."

"Good."

I watched as he hurried out of bed and pulled his pants on.

"How far apart are the contraction?" he asked, glancing over his shoulder at me.

I looked at the alarm clock. "I don't know. Ten minutes?"

"Is that good or bad?"

I gasped as the pain became more intense. "Both." I was done being pregnant. I wanted the baby out. I was just shy of thirty-nine weeks and was as big as a house.

"Why didn't you wake me earlier?"

"I wasn't sure if it was time or not."

"But, it is?"

"Oh, yeah."

"Should I bring you to the hospital?"

"No. We're having the baby here," I reminded him.

He frowned. "What if there's complications?"

We'd had the same argument over and over. Ransom was so worried that they'd need to do surgery, especially since the baby was so big. But, Dr. Frazer had assured me that it was normal. Especially since Ransom himself was a bigger guy. "Everything will be fine."

He grabbed his cell phone. "Okay. Just keep breathing. I'll make the call."

Nodding, I relaxed as the contraction subsided, knowing the relief would be short-lived. Not to mention that every time they returned, the pain was much stronger. "Tell him to bring me something for the pain."

"Yeah, I will."

After hanging up with the doctor, Ransom asked if he should boil water or bring me something to bite on.

"Boil water?"

"That's what they say to do in the movies," he said with a sheepish grin.

"Just bring in some towels," I replied. "This is going to get messy. In fact… Oh, God. My water just broke."

His face paled.

"Is the doctor coming?" I asked.

"Yeah. He will be here in twenty minutes. Tops."

I watched Ransom leave the bedroom and closed my eyes, mentally preparing myself for the next contraction while practicing my breathing. He returned in a few seconds, carrying a pile of towels while talking to someone else on the phone. As I was listening, another contraction hit.

"Ransom!" I bellowed.

"Gotta go," he said, hanging up.

"I have to push," I said, the urge suddenly hitting me.

"What? The doctor isn't here yet. Aren't you supposed to wait until you're fully dilated?"

Had I not been in so much pain, I would have laughed at him. The big, strong Alpha Lycan looked more like a frightened rabbit at that moment. "Maybe… I… am… fully dilated."

"You don't know?"

I shook my head.

"Should I check?"

I knew he was trying to help, but Ransom would have no idea of what to do down there. Not medically, at least.

I swore under my breath. "No. Just… oh, God… I really have to push… Come here."

He winced as I squeezed his hand. "Hailey."

"What?" I asked between gasps of air.

"Your grip. It's pretty… " Seeing the look on my face, his voice trailed off.

I loved the man to death, but right then and there, I was ready to rip his head off.

"You want to know what *hurts*?" I growled. "Giving birth to a damn watermelon, Ransom. The one you put inside of me…"

"Sorry, squeeze as hard as you need to. Give it all you got."

"I think… the baby is… coming."

His eyes widened in horror. "What? *Now*? The doctor's not here."

"I know. Just… stay with me."

"I'd never leave you, Hailey. Especially with that death grip of yours," he said, a smile in his voice. "I couldn't run if I wanted to."

I glared at him.

Fifteen minutes later, after enduring the most excruciating pain in my life, our son was born.

"A boy," Ransom announced, his voice thick with emotion.

He held up the baby and my eyes filled with tears. My heart seemed to overflow with happiness.

Ransom began wiping the blood off of him with a towel. "He sure is quiet. Is that normal? I thought they were supposed to cry?"

My chest tightened. "Is he breathing?"

"Let me look at him," called out Dr. Frazer, now racing into the bedroom. He grabbed the infant and before either one of us could say another word, the baby was crying.

"How does he look?" I asked, able to breathe again.

"As far as I can tell, he's as healthy as a horse. Good job, Ransom. Is this your first delivery?" teased the doctor as he handed me the baby.

Ransom smiled weakly. "What gave it away?"

"Nothing, actually. Looks like you did pretty damn good," the doctor replied. "Both of you."

I stared down into our son's face and fell immediately in love with him. He had a light layer of jet-black hair and dark eyes. "Shh… Drake. It's okay."

Hearing my voice, the baby quieted down.

"Here. Wrap him in this," the doctor said, producing a soft blanket. "We'll give him a bath after I check you over and make sure you're okay."

"Okay. Look at him. Isn't he adorable?" I murmured, swaddling Drake in the blanket.

Ransom leaned down and touched Drake's cheek fondly. "He's perfect."

"A big guy, too," Dr, Frazer said. "I'd say he weighs over nine pounds."

"Good thing, too. He's going to be the Alpha of our clan one day," Ransom replied. "Strong and powerful."

The doctor, who was also Lycan and a new clan member, chuckled. "Damn right he will be. Oh, that reminds me, Ransom. I wanted you to know that those tests we took… there's nothing to worry about. In fact, you seem to be as healthy as a horse as well. Whatever was ailing Travis and Jordan isn't showing up in your bloodwork."

"What about being able to stop myself from shifting, mid-point?" Ransom asked.

"It's not unheard of. I've met other shifters who are able to do the same thing. It takes a lot of strength, which you obviously have."

Ransom and I both breathed a sigh of relief.

"Do you have any idea of what was wrong with them?" I asked.

"Personally, I believe that it was just some kind of genetic anomaly. Just be grateful that it skipped you, Ransom."

"What about Drake?" I replied. "Could he have it?"

The doctor sighed. "It's always possible. You'll just have to keep an eye on him as he grows up. If we're lucky, it will skip him, too."

"Let's hope." Ransom reached over and stroked Drake's dark hair fondly.

A short time later, after Drake was washed and bundled back up again in my arms, there was a knock on the door.

"Is it safe to enter?" called a voice. Reece.

"Yeah, come on in," Ransom called out.

He walked in, carrying an oversized teddy bear. Behind him was Malone, holding a box of cigars.

"Girl or boy?" Reece asked as they approached.

"Boy. Just like I knew it would be," Ransom said, puffing out his chest.

The two men stopped at the edge of the bed, both smiling.

"Congratulations," Reece said, staring down at our son.

"Yeah, great job," Malone said. "He looks like a healthy little bugger."

"Big bugger," corrected Ransom. "Drake weighs nine pounds, six ounces."

"Is that large?" Malone replied.

"Yes. I take it you never had any kids?" I asked him.

I knew that Reece had a daughter, much older than us. He also had a new lady in his life—woman from our clan named Betty who he'd met at our wedding. Malone was a different story, however. In fact, nobody knew much about Malone's private life.

He smirked. "Hell, maybe. I have no idea."

"You're still young enough to have a real family of your own," the doctor said.

"The clan *is* my family. Most of them act like kids, so I don't need my own." He quickly changed the subject. "You smoke, Doc? I brought along some cigars."

"Now and again," he replied.

"No problem." Malone passed out the cigars. "I brought some scotch, too. The good kind." He winked at Ransom. "Figured you'll be doing a lot of drinking once Drake turns sixteen and starts driving. May as well get you ready now."

Ransom smiled. "No doubt."

"So, how are things going with the clan?" Malone asked.

"Good," he replied. "For the most part."

"Rumor has spread that you're doing a good job," Reece said, beaming at him.

"I've heard the same thing," Malone said, placing his hand on Ransom's shoulder. "I'm glad you stepped up to the plate and did what had to be done."

"Me, too," admitted Ransom. "Things seem to be falling into place."

The guys talked a little more about the clan and plans for the future. Meanwhile, I started getting really sleepy and could tell that Drake was starting to get feisty.

"I should probably try feeding him," I said, when there was a break in the conversation. "Why don't you guys go outside and have your cigars and scotch?"

"You need any help?" Ransom asked.

I laughed. "Feeding, Drake? No. I think I'm good there."

He leaned down and gave me a kiss. "Text me if you need anything."

I nodded.

"I'll be back in a couple of minutes," Dr. Frazer said. "Then I'll take him so you can get some rest."

"Thank you," I replied.

The four left the room and I began breastfeeding Drake. It was harder and a lot more painful than I'd imagined, but after a couple of minutes, I managed to get the hang of it.

"What do you say, Drake?" I murmured, staring down at him lovingly. "Are you going to follow in your daddy's footsteps one day and be an Alpha of your own clan?"

Drake's eyes met mine.

I stared deeply into them, hoping that life gave him everything he deserved. I didn't care if he was Alpha or ended up doing his own thing when he got older. I just wanted him safe, healthy, and… sane.

As if somehow understanding, his eyes lit up for a second and then grew drowsy again.

I smiled and began to hum *Rock-a-bye Baby*. Right then and there, I had everything I could ever want—a loving husband and a child I already adored. My life was such a far cry from the year before, when I'd been terrified and running from my fears. Now, here I was turning another chapter in my life and excited to see what the future held for the three of us. Although I knew there'd be ups-and-downs, nothing would ever come between us. And damn any one, or *thing,* who tried.

"Right, Drake?" I whispered, bringing him to my shoulder. I patted his back gently and smiled when he let out a large burp. "Yeah… I knew you'd agree."

The End

Printed in Great Britain
by Amazon